4/21

Also by Susan Conley

*Elsey Come Home*
*Stop Here, This Is the Place*
*Paris Was the Place*
*The Foremost Good Fortune*

# LANDSLIDE

# *LANDSLIDE*

*Susan Conley*

Alfred A. Knopf   New York   2021

THIS IS A BORZOI BOOK
PUBLISHED BY ALFRED A. KNOPF

www.aaknopf.com

Knopf, Borzoi Books, and the colophon are registered trademarks of Penguin Random House LLC.

Library of Congress Cataloging-in-Publication Data
Names: Conley, Susan, [date] author.
Title: Landslide / Susan Conley.
Description: New York : Alfred A. Knopf, 2021.
Identifiers: LCCN 2020013109 | ISBN 9780525657132 (hardcover) |
    ISBN 9780525657149 (ebook)
Classification: LCC PS3603.O5365 L36 2021 | DDC 813/.6—dc23
LC record available at https://lccn.loc.gov/2020013109

Jacket photographs: (boy) Charlie Bonallack / Millennium Images, U.K.;
    (water) Chris Meredith / Moment / Getty Images
Jacket design by Kelly Blair

Manufactured in the United States of America
First Edition

*For My Mother, For Everything*

Boys enter the house, boys enter the house.
Boys, and with them the idea of boys (ideas leaden,
reductive, inflexible), enter the house . . . Boys enter
the house speaking nonsense. Boys enter the house
calling for mother.

RICK MOODY, "BOYS"


Yes, I am home again, but home has changed.

MAY SARTON, *Letters from Maine*

## PART ONE

# HOW TO TALK TO WOLVES

IT'S LATE AFTERNOON AT the end of a long October when the Fleetwood Mac song comes on. We're halfway down the peninsula, and I tell the wolves I was raised on Stevie Nicks, so could they please let me listen to the whole thing. Because Sam, the younger one, has a bad habit of changing the station.

"Mom," he says in his deadpan and stares out the cracked windshield. "I *already knew that* about you growing up on Stevie Nicks."

He's sixteen and gangly, with poking collarbones like little car door handles. He wants to be a professional basketball player, but will settle for rock musician. His face has grown long and gaunt, so he doesn't look like himself but the person he's in the process of becoming.

I tell myself it's a beautiful face. It's important to tell myself that many things about teenage boys are beautiful so I don't panic.

The song's about a woman who climbs a mountain at the end of a love affair and sees her reflection in the snow-covered hills and becomes less afraid. It's in a challenging register for me, so I'm almost crowing while I sing. But for many months I've wanted to be less afraid, and I feel for a moment like Stevie Nicks is a close friend. Like she knows me.

"Every time I turn on the radio," Sam says in his most sarcastic voice, "it's Stevie the Good Witch of the West Nicks. The thing is, Mom, I don't want to grow up in Maine on Fleetwood Mac *like you did.*"

His hair is the color of straw and hangs below his ears, and I can't tell if the hair is a joke or a bad fashion statement that involves rarely washing it. But I grin at him and move my head to the beat, because at least he's speaking. Sometimes my son's silence in the car is flammable.

Charlie's in the backseat. He's our moral police. Seventeen going on something like thirty-three. He thinks sports are a hoax and believes in the laws of physics and a senior named Lucy who recently moved to Maine from Burundi. He's taller and sturdier than Sam and has my husband's dark, wavy hair that doesn't move even in high winds.

I am trying not to think about my husband. He is renowned on the peninsula for his gargantuan energy and for being a fisherman who doesn't come home empty-handed. Ten days ago his boat engine exploded off Georges Bank and he broke his right femur and got airlifted to a hospital in Nova Scotia, where he's recovering from surgery.

I'm not allowed to talk to the boys about how much I miss him. I'm not allowed to talk to the boys about my dread or my worry or any of my emotions, really. This isn't because the boys aren't emotional. It's just that no outward expression of emotion is sanctioned in this phase of wolf development.

I've still somehow convinced myself that I am needed more here with them than with my husband. Even though the boys answer most of my questions in monosyllables. Since I got back from the hospital two days ago, I have not been able to take my eyes off them.

The tourists have all left, so there are no other cars on the road. Just a fading sun that knives through the pine trees and puts its little spell on me. I keep asking myself who I want to be. For Kit and Sam and Charlie. It's a coping strategy I read about in the hospital last week. Who do you want to be for the people who need you? Kit told me last week he didn't know who he was anymore now that he couldn't fish. The newspapers write about all the real estate money pouring into our state and how good the restaurants are. But most fishermen I know are selling their trawlers and fending off lenders, and I began making a film about this a year ago. About how almost none of the fishermen here can afford to fish anymore. It's my fourth documentary.

"You think you know me," I say to the boys. "But you might not know all of me."

"Oh, we know you, Mom." Sam turns and rolls his eyes at his older brother like I'm a nut job.

He's wearing the Adidas T-shirt with the logo of the green leaf on the pocket, which he's convinced is marijuana. The shirt has some mysterious dime-sized stains, and is way too big, so he looks like someone not getting enough nutrition or hygiene.

*"Mom. Please."* Charlie's trying to sound like he and I are the adults in the car. He had debate team today, and the button-down shirt he's wearing is permanently scarred with wrinkles. The look is young mad scientist.

I love this song and the boys in this car being forced to listen to this song. I turn it up really loud, the way I used to when I was a different person and did not have two wolves.

The contract you make when you're with a fisherman is that he will go fish. Kit has left me on our island to fish almost every week since I married him. But he'd been gone three months before the accident, and I think the boys and I have missed him so much we cannot say. Tall and lanky, with steady blue eyes. My loner with a thousand friends.

The whole crew was badly injured in the explosion—Kit's cousin Dyer, plus the two younger guys and the woman with the tattoo who Dyer hired to be the cook. All of them got serious burns and broken bones, but Kit's the only one still in the hospital.

Thank you that none of them died. Thank you. Thank you. Thank you. It's rare you get an engine explosion and someone doesn't die.

Since Kit got hurt, it's been a clothing pageant at our house. The boys wear his old sweaters and baseball hats and fight over who gets his boots when they bail the boats. Their allegiance to their father is not surprising. A man who puts great value on being steady. He can't walk to the general store in the village he grew up in without stopping to talk to everyone he sees. This has always been part of loving him—the people he collects—and I've made my peace with it. But he doesn't show his complicated emotions even to me.

When Kit called the boys from the hospital the first time, he said they needed to listen to me while he got better, and that they were lucky to have a mother who loved them like I did. I was standing next to his electronic bed, and I smiled, but what I was really thinking was what would become of my husband if he could not fish.

THREE MONTHS APART IS a short expanse of time or very long. Marriage has a way of contracting and expanding like this, and you can lose track of what is real time and what's fabricated time. But since Kit went to Nova Scotia, I've felt more alone than I did the other times he's been gone.

I hadn't wanted him to leave. I told him this. I knew our separation would feel more concrete, because he'd be away much longer this time. And this is what happened. I became caught up with the film and with the wolves, and perhaps I tried to temporarily replace my husband with these things.

It looks like an omen now, because he was injured. But what I wanted was for him to sell his boat. I didn't tell him this. I couldn't in the end. It's too hard to make a living fishing in Maine, and it's not always about lack of fish. It's about lack of quota—the number of fish you're allowed to catch—and it's about lack of fish processors and buyers. But really in the end it's about price, which is so low right now it's killing Kit.

His cousin Dyer had the swordfish boat and the longline license in Nova Scotia. Kit made a speech to me about providing for his family before he left. It was a matter of pride for him to go. Which was also a matter of money. When is marriage not in some way a question of money? I think once you start worrying about money, you don't stop.

"Mom," Charlie says. "The voice, Mom. *Please.*"

We pass Kit's uncle's gun shop with the black vinyl siding, and the trailer on the hill next to the gun shop where one of the older cousins lives who's trying to scrape by off clamming. But no one can really live off clamming here anymore because of the red tide and the closures.

"What are you doing with your mouth, Mom?" Sam puts his phone in his lap and stares at me. This is rare, that he actually sees me.

The sign outside the grange hall reads BEAN SUPPER FRIDAY AT FIVE.

"With my *mouth?*" Now he's worried about my mouth?

"Yeah. Moving your lips like that."

How to talk to the wolves. This is often the question. With their splotchy faces and tree-bark smell and bones growing longer in their sleep.

"I'm singing to myself, so that you guys can't hear me."

"That's strange, Mom. Please stop. Please don't do that. Please just sing *normally.*"

I don't ask Sam how I can sing normally when I'm not allowed to sing at all.

For a long time it was my joke at church and at the library and at my sister-in-law Candy's store that my boys were not the kind who would turn on me. Candy tells me the important thing is not to take any of what teenagers do personally. She's three years older than Kit and is Sewall village's unofficial mayor. She says it's a phase with my boys—their need to separate from me.

She's lived in Sewall her whole life, and she has one boy and two girls, all of them grown. She says it's bad with the girls too, but different. You know more what the girls are thinking. Maybe the pain of separation comes on faster with them, and they become your friend again sooner.

Boys can be harder to read, she says. You have to pay close attention. The boys will say they're okay when they're really suffering or have become secret delinquents. "But no matter what," Candy says, "no one will love you more or be meaner to you than your own kids."


PAY ATTENTION, JILL, I tell myself. Pay attention to the road.

My mother used to accuse me of not paying attention because I could hold two conversations at once. The one inside my head and the one everyone else listened to. This was in Harwich, the mill town two hours north of here where I grew up.

Sam can do it too. Hold two conversations in his head at once. Sometimes he appears lost in the ether. It makes me want to grab his attention. But he has a name for mothers who appear too eager—ones who coddle or cheer too hard at their basketball games. He calls them try-hards, and please let this never be me.

It's difficult not to try hard with Sam. But the boys want me to *chill.* They use this word maybe a half dozen times a day.

"You don't know that I went to the prom with Jamie Rogers and we listened to this song on the drive home. He wore a white tuxedo." I'm trying to hold their attention, because it's a glorious thing when they give it to me. The ocean follows the car like a conscience, telling me to turn the car around and go back to the hospital.

Charlie stretches his legs out between the front seats. "You went to the prom with someone who wore a white tuxedo? That's pretty cheesy, Mom."

"This whole Fleetwood Mac album," I say, "is so good. Never forget it."

"*Never.*" Sam smiles, and changes the station on me.

But I've already won the afternoon because he's still talking.

I PARK THE SUBARU under the pine trees. Then follow the boys down to the dock, where we tie up the rowboat and *The Duchess,* our beat-up skiff with the 15-horsepower Evinrude, which we take back and forth to the island. I remind Charlie to go slow because the water has more chop than yesterday. I'd love not to get wet.

It takes four minutes to cross the channel to our island. It is not really our island. It's Kit's family's island by way of eminent domain or maybe squatters' rights, going back to his ancestors who got off the boat from Ireland with harpoons. And it's possibly the most beautiful place in the world.

The northern end, closest to the house, is made of thick slabs of dark granite, which gradually narrow like the tip of a spear. At low tide you can jump from ledge to ledge here, and the ocean leaves a little pool inside the rocks where we swim. The house is a gray-shingled saltbox with a high pitched roof in the shape of an *A.* It sits on the ledge above the spear with the feathery grasses and blueberry bushes and patches of silver-green moss.

Inside there's a galley kitchen and shelves crammed with bowls and plates and old crayon drawings of fish. The plywood counter is crowded with bright boxes of tea and jars of granola and beans. The woodstove sits to the right of the counter. We make sure to have enough wood, so it never goes out now. The couch sits between the woodstove and the ladder to the loft that Kit built after the boys were born. The couch is made of green velvet and is too fancy to be here.

The story goes that Kit's mother liked living on the island so much she made Kit's father, Jimmy, bring the couch out on his lobster boat. Martha had gotten the couch from her mother, who'd gotten the couch from her mother.

Martha died when Kit was ten. He does not ever talk about it, so it's something we hardly speak of. But yesterday, when the wind slammed us from the north and it felt so raw out, Charlie and Sam and I sat on the couch with blankets and tea, and I thanked Martha for the couch again in my mind and wondered how long Sam will make us stay here.

The last five Novembers we've moved to Jimmy's house on the mainland to wait out the winter, and Jimmy's driven to a rental condo in Daytona Beach. But Sam says he won't leave the island until Kit gets home from the hospital, and Jimmy announced that he's not going anywhere until Kit comes back either.

SAM'S LYING ON THE couch with his hands over his eyes now. Never a good sign.

He says he has an essay to write.

"Something descriptive, Mom. It also has to have *purpose*."

"Oh God. How long?" It's important to try and act calm.

I know he's waiting for any excuse to divert the blame to me. Then his story can be not that he didn't plan ahead on the assignment but that I've caused him to feel so bad about procrastinating that he can't possibly write the essay.

"Five pages."

"Due when?" I smile. Just please don't make it be due tomorrow.

"Tomorrow, like I said."

He didn't say.

He keeps his hands over his eyes so he doesn't have to look at me.

"Oh, Sam."

I can't understand why he didn't mention the essay in the car or the boat or while we just ate the enchiladas. I cannot.

"It's fine, Mom. Chill, please. Really. It's okay."

"What is it even meant to be *about*?" I don't try to explain how angry I am. We have been through this many times. He knows.

He was born two months premature and lived in the neonatal intensive care at Maine Medical Center in Portland for several weeks while his little lungs grew, and Charlie says I baby him. He's probably right and that my instinct for this started at the hospital. But two years ago Sam's best friend, Liam, drowned.

It happened at the beginning of basketball season, when Liam and Sam were in eighth grade and spacy and goofy and just starting what they called their first rock band.

Each day after basketball practice they walked across the bridge that connects Sewall to Avery to get a ride home from Kit at Dairy Queen. I thought they walked on the sidewalk on top of the bridge that's protected from the cars by a high green metal railing. You can look down from there and see the brick part of Avery, where the high school is.

But what the boys did was climb underneath the bridge and walk on the railroad tracks, suspended over the water in all this metal caging. There was a gap between two of the wooden ties. A break where a boy could fall through. This is what happened to Liam. He fell.

There is no other way to say this. I have gone over it and over it, scouring it for more information, and there is none. He fell.

It took almost everyone we know who owns a boat searching

for two days in the high seas before they found his body. May he rest in peace.

He was a beautiful boy, with almond skin like his father's and a photographic memory for song lyrics. Name a song. Once, after he'd started playing Kit's album collection in the house, he told me that the band he and Sam had started was going to sing complicated harmonies like Tom Petty and the Heartbreakers. Sam on guitar, their friend Robbie on piano, and Liam on drums and vocals.

Liam and Sam had the same longish dark blond hair and the same way of leaning their heads slightly to the left when they laughed. People confused them from the back. Liam's mother, Sally, told me last month that her young girls still see Sam at school and think he's Liam.

Sally and her husband, Jorge, own a vegetable farm on the peninsula, with gardens that go all the way down to the ocean. It's become a destination, this farm. We all stood in their biggest field and said goodbye to Liam in the most moving ceremony. Sally asked people to share stories of him and what he meant to them, and Sam was silent the whole time. He told me afterward that he'd wanted to say many things about his friend but he couldn't speak.

Sam became afraid of falling after that. You could see it in his body. Tense in his shoulders, like he was going to fall off the boat or the float or the house. He'd lived through something so big on the bridge and couldn't explain it to us. I did not know what he was thinking. I wondered constantly what he'd told himself about what he'd seen.

There was an anxiety that crept into almost everything he did, and I saw how much he needed me and didn't want to need me. When he finally went back to school, he met with the school social worker in her office with the brown corduroy couch and told her that he should have drowned, not Liam. He said he didn't feel like he had a self anymore now that Liam had died.

Sam had many sessions with Nettie. She was a twenty-six-year-old recent graduate of the University of Maine's School of Social Work, with a deceptively casual way of speaking to teenagers that got them to confide in her. She told me once that Sam said he felt so alone after the drowning he was almost suffocating in the aloneness.

It was Kit's and my job, Nettie said, to validate him. This meant we had to tell him things like he was not alone and he did not have to be strong.

Nettie said many of the kids she saw at school needed this kind of attention and were not good at asking for it. Lots of the boys had distorted ideas of what being strong and being masculine meant, and they suffered when they didn't need to.

I told Sam, *I am here.* And, *This is real, this sadness you're going through. I'm going to help you however I can.*

Nettie said even if he pretended not to hear us, some of it would get through. I think this has been true, though it hasn't been easy to get Kit to understand how to do it, and I know Sam hasn't always felt understood. Maybe that's the job of teenagers, to feel misunderstood by their parents.

Sam never cried in front of us after Liam died. When I asked him about this, he said Jimmy told him that real men don't cry. Only weak ones.

Jimmy is a short, bearded gnome of a man with piercing eyes who hauls six hundred lobster traps a day and appraises people based on physical strength. It has been my job to help Sam unlearn many of the ideas about manhood that Jimmy has taught him.

During the first weeks, Sam slept on a blow-up mattress on

the floor next to our bed on the island. Twice he woke us up yelling for Liam in his sleep. Then he moved back up to the loft and refused to talk about it anymore. So the sadness became something he keeps to himself.

We often try to guess what he's feeling now. But I think the biggest mistake I make with Sam is to assume he isn't feeling things just because he's not talking.

You could say he grew up when Liam drowned, but that would make it sound too easy. He was only fourteen. Boys don't become men overnight. Sam has a willingness to self-sabotage that he didn't have before Liam died. This is what Nettie calls it. And he goes through new phases of not talking. But there's this emotion inside him that wants to come out, which is why I'll help him with his essay.

"It's supposed to be an essay on American hubris. Whatever that means." He's still got his hands over his eyes while he talks so he looks like me when the boys make me watch a horror movie with them on the laptop.

"Hubris?" Charlie says through the door that separates the living room from my bedroom. He likes to do his homework in there on my bed. Says it's quieter and he can get a break from us. "Sam has a lot of it."

"Of what?" I'm over at the sink trying to scrub what's left of the enchiladas in the baking pan.

"Of hubris," Charlie says.

"Charlie, please shut up." Sam sits up.

"It means he thinks highly of himself!" Charlie laughs at his joke, but there's nothing funny about Sam writing an essay.

"Enough," I say. "Charlie, you know we can't stand it when you try to talk to us through the door. Please do your homework or go clean up the mess in the bathroom."

He's been trying out a home experiment involving what he calls salinity and electrical conductivity, which means vats of ocean water spilled on the bathroom floor and lots of black rubber tubing.

"What about Dad?" I tell Sam. "You could write about Dad and his accident."

"It has to have *conflict,* Mom. Something in the essay has to show a *change* or something."

"I think many things have changed since Dad's been gone."

I don't add that I believe any time three humans are asked to live together on a small island in a former fishing shack with bad, really expensive electric-baseboard heat, where at night it gets down to twenty-five degrees and where the fourth human in the house is in another country recovering from surgery, it will require the humans to be willing to change. Maybe Sam most of all.

"Just so I have this right." I try to keep my voice upbeat. "This essay is really due *tomorrow?*"

Please let me go to bed. I don't want to help write a high school essay on hubris.

I grab the empty water glasses from the table and carry them to the sink. Outside the sky and sea are black, and my heart sinks. We don't mind the cold in Sewall. We don't mind the rain or snow, but we mind the early dark in October.

"Yeah, and I really need your help."

"Why do you do this? Why do you wait and tyrannize me?" I sit down on the rug and stare into the metal slat on the woodstove where you can see the flames.

"I can't even say that word. It's like a Shakespeare word, Mom." A flap of hair hangs down over his eye like a little flag. "Who actually *believes* in Shakespeare anyway? Who actually believes in *school?*"

"I think you should actually go to bed. I don't think nine o'clock is the right time to start a five-page essay."

I try to stay calm. The upbeatness is getting harder.

"I think you go to bed, and you tell Mrs. Curtis in the morning that you need an extension through the weekend, and that you're very sorry things got away from you."

"Things *got away from me*? Thanks, Mom. This is the *one thing* I need your help on." He stands and puts his hands on his narrow hips. "Thanks *a lot.*"

"I *am* helping you. But not tonight. Tonight you need to apologize."

He goes into the kitchen and opens the fridge and gazes into it like it holds the clue to his future. "Apologize for what?"

"For being cruel to me. I do not allow cruel."

"I can't take it anymore." He rests his head on the fridge door.

"Take what?"

"The girls. They answer everything in class. They have their hands up all the time. I can't keep up. I'm never going to school again."

This is another one of his strategies. To divert the conversation away from him to something only tangentially related to what we're arguing about.

"Don't worry about the girls. The girls know everything now. Later, if they're like me, the patriarchy will start to wear them down and they won't be sure they know anything."

He rolls his eyes. "Please, please, no more speeches."

I point to the ladder. "To bed now."

He stares at me, then smiles and opens his arms out wide. "Let's hug it out, Jillian."

He only calls me Jillian when he wants my attention or pity. It makes me crazy.

But then he comes to the couch and leans down and puts his arms around me. I don't say anything.

"You're so thin. When did you get this skinny?" It's like he's discovering me for the first time in weeks.

If he would let me hug him like this each night, I'd never worry about him again.

"Do we like have any food in here?" He walks back toward the fridge.

"We just finished dinner. Please don't get out more food. Please just go to bed."

Did we really just hug?

"But I'm starving." He gets the jar of peanut butter down from the shelf and takes a spoon from the drawer under the counter. "I'm starving, and there's like no food here."

AFTER SAM CLIMBS UP to the loft, I lie on the couch and look at his Instagram. He's posted a video of the best NBA dunks of 2019. And then a photo of himself in the passenger seat of a brown sedan outside McDonald's, smoking what appears to be a thinly rolled joint. *#feelingIrie #RastamanVibration* My skin starts to feel prickly.

I GET VERY LITTLE sleep after that. At three in the morning I break down and plug the space heater in. When I wake for good, it's still dark out and I see Kit alone in his hospital room.

I'm still getting pieces of information about the boat, but I know there was water vapor in the gas line and then someone lit a cigarette. Kit was in the bow fixing a cable and got thrown in the explosion. His right femur broke, and when they got him to the hospital they found the internal bleeding.

The call came while I was in the village filming Woody Gilman down on Jimmy's wharf. Woody is probably Jimmy's closest friend, a lobsterman with the bushiest silver eyebrows, who demands your full attention. He told me that his catch was off 40 percent this year because the lobsters were staying out in the deeper fathoms. He said he knows men now who get up at 2 a.m. and drive their boats seventy miles out to sea to haul traps. "We can pretend climate change is just political," he told me, "but everyone knows the water's warming."

He got a call on his cell phone then from his wife, Edna, who's been Sewall's postmistress for thirty years. Woody always takes Edna's calls. It was eleven in the morning, and I got out my own phone. I was distracted by the things Woody had said—thinking about the lobsters and all the fish that have stopped migrating, and I had this sense of my own inaction again. Such regret about the warming water. But I was also in denial over it.

I played the message on my phone, and a man's voice said my

husband was gravely injured but would likely make it through the night. I needed to come right away.

The feeling I had was not unlike the feeling when Kit called from Dairy Queen to say Liam had fallen off the bridge. This sick kind of dread. But also the sensation that it wasn't real. That it was not happening.

I drove seven hours with a terrible pressure on the back of my skull, but I did not think I'd find an injured man when I got to the hospital.

It was only when I saw Kit in the bed with the IV line and the oxygen tube going into his nose that I understood. They had his right leg suspended over the bed with this pulley system, and even then it took me several more hours before I really got the scope of his injuries.

I think the nurses thought I was crying because of how bad Kit looked, and that was a big part of it. But I'd also just missed him so much. His eyes were closed and his face was calm, the skin pale in a way I'd never seen. He'd lost a lot of blood by then and looked thinner too, his lined face more chiseled, the bones almost closer to the surface of the skin.

The first thing he said when he woke up was that he couldn't believe I'd come.

I said *of course* I came.

He said I should have come sooner.

I said I came as fast as I could.

Then he said he should have made more money and that his way of life was ending.

He was delirious. On the verge maybe of some mental collapse. The blue in his eyes was darker. It was like something had broken loose in him. He was at sea in his mind and I was with him, but I was only watching.

His hair fell down over his forehead, and he looked like a replica of Charlie in the bed but also Sam, though how it was possible that he resembled both boys so closely when the boys are so distinct with their different coloring and shapes of their faces is still unclear to me.

I gave him my full attention and tried to forget the boys and any of the world outside the hospital. I tried to concentrate only on him. I watched everything the nurses and doctors did to him closely. Every procedure.

I know now that the femur is the largest bone in the body, and that when it breaks the pain is agonizing. The nurses gave my husband several different pain meds to help him sleep that first night before the surgery, and I think Dilaudid worked best. But I knew nothing about traumatic injuries then or what they can do to you.

The head nurse, Linda, came in to check on him often. She had dark skin and many beautiful, long, orange-colored braids that she pulled back in a black elastic headband, and she was very calm with Kit. Very intentional. She told me, "Injuries like this change people. Don't be surprised if he seems different for a while. Sadder, even. The man has seen a whole lot in the last day."

DURING THE SURGERY THE next morning, they cleaned the bone and the muscles around it to help stop any infection. Then they inserted a metal rod into the center of the bone to support the bone while it healed. There were no fragments surrounding the break, so none of the blood vessels had been damaged, thank God. Such a relief. And they were able to position the bones to fuse again.

When he was back in his room afterward, he woke up and looked at me every few hours, searching my face. But I knew he wasn't really there. I could not believe how frail he seemed, and how much older. But I tried to make my face into my normal face whenever he opened his eyes, so that he wouldn't see my shock.

Time slowed that day. It was a deep, greenish-black ocean at high tide, and Kit kept sleeping these dead sleeps and waking up with drug-fueled announcements. Around eight that night he looked at me. "You're here? When did you come?"

I took his hand. "I've been here the whole time, baby."

"Not true. I always know when you're here."

He asked me where the boys were.

I told him that I'd left them at Jimmy's until he was through the surgery and feeling stronger, then I'd bring them.

"I just want to see their faces. I really, really need to see them."

He didn't say anything else for a minute, and I thought he was sleeping again. But then he said, "Who ever thought fishing would end in my lifetime?"

"It's not over yet." I bent down and kissed the side of his face. "You got hurt pretty bad. You got pretty injured."

I worried that my tears might scare him. Then he'd know how dangerous the accident had been. But of course he knew. He knows everything about boats and engine explosions. He'd lost two friends that way.

His room had a heavy, laminate door that led to a little bathroom, and after he fell back asleep I went into this bathroom and stared in the mirror and tried to be honest. I told myself that things would need to change. They would have to. I mean, how could he ever fish again? He could not even walk. What was there for him to return to?

He woke up later that night and said he needed me.

He never usually said these kinds of things explicitly, and it made me smile and I could feel the solidity of our marriage. But it also disconcerted me, because these things were not him. Not the him that I knew.

He said he hoped I could forgive him.

What did he want me to forgive him for except for coming to Nova Scotia? I could not blame him for that. It had to be the Dilaudid.

I told him that I'd pull the boys from school and camp out in his room if it would help him get better faster.

He said I was crazy. The boys needed school.

THE SURGEON CAME BY the next morning while Kit was asleep. A tall, reedy, condescending man with sand-colored eyes who removed his bifocals and told me that he believed in early, partial weight-bearing on Kit's leg. He said Kit would need to move several times a day and that the physical therapist would come to see him in the afternoon.

Then he paused and looked right at me and said my husband was lucky.

"Lucky how?" I asked.

"Your husband has been in a terrible accident. Did you not realize?"

It took a lot for me not to tell him to stop talking to me like I was a child.

He said we were lucky the boat hadn't sunk.

Then he put the glasses back on and nodded at me and left.

When Kit woke up the next time, it was almost noon and I was sitting in the reclining chair covered in green synthetic material. I slept in this chair, and sometimes I read in this chair, or stared at my husband in the blue light of the machinery. But I was crying a little this time, and I tried to wipe away the tears before he saw them. He'd caught me by surprise.

He looked thin and gray in the bed, as if all the life had been sucked out of him. I tried not to show it on my face, but it was the most extraordinary thing. My husband, who could take up a room.

"Jilly." He really stared at me for what felt like the first time since I'd gotten to the hospital.

It felt good to finally be seen like this.

But then he said, "Please don't get heavy on me. I can't do this if you get heavy."

And I didn't feel seen at all. I thought maybe he and I had grown apart while he'd been gone. Or that he really was a different person since the accident. That he'd changed, like Linda had warned me.

THE DAY BEFORE KIT left for Nova Scotia, he took us to the Sedgewick cliffs, which only the locals know about. You have to steer *The Duchess* through a narrow gut in the rocks, then anchor and swim in, and these cliffs always make me nervous. They're high and steep and you need to jump as far out as you can to clear them.

Charlie went first. I remember the ocean was so clear that day that I could see his body really well underneath the water, and I watched it rise to the surface.

Kit whooped on his way down and smacked the water with his hand when he came up.

Then Sam was alone on the cliff.

"No wimps!" Charlie yelled to him.

I leaned over the side of the boat and told Charlie that I'd kill him if he made Sam jump. *I will kill you.*

"God, Mom, chill!" He tried to splash me with water.

"No, *you* chill. Do you want your brother to get hurt?"

It was a big deal for Sam to jump. If he jumped, maybe it would mean he'd overcome his worst fears about Liam.

Kit climbed into the boat and put his arms around me in the stern, so now I was soaking wet too. "Jilly, please stop protecting him."

He'd been telling me this for years. I could not hear him. I did not want to.

"You're good, right?" he whispered. "You're going to be good."

He meant while he was away on Dyer's boat, but I wanted him to name it. That he was really going. Because all of us, Sam and Charlie and I, know too much about being left behind by Kit. He says he fishes for *us,* but I wonder.

I could never tell Kit these things. If I did, he'd completely disagree. He likes to hug us and to pick the boys up off the floor. He's really physical in this way. He likes to pound his chest when he gets emotional and say, "In here. I feel it in here!" Like we *know* what he's feeling. But we don't really know, because he doesn't say.

I think we understand the love he has for us, and the need he has to believe he's protecting us. But a lot of the time the boys and I are protecting ourselves, because he's gone.

I don't know what he'd do if he didn't fish. This is not hypothetical. What if you take Kit off his boat and take him off the ocean? I don't know if he can change like that. I don't know if any of the fishermen I've talked to can. Or what the price will be.

His plan was to go to Georges Bank for weeks at a time, then back to port to stay at Dyer's house. Then out again. The season is relentless. I'd thought of driving the boys up in August, but Sam was already working hard for Shorty, and Charlie was hoping for an internship at a hospital lab in Portland. So I didn't see how I could make it happen.

I had the urge to ask Kit to stay home and sell the *Jillian Lynne* and go to community college with the money the state was offering fishermen willing to start over. But I didn't dare.

While we waited for Sam to jump, he told me again how much he wanted us to come up and that if the boys were too busy, I should come on my own. "Could you please do that?" he said. "Please come."

I knew he would feel alone in Nova Scotia each time the boat went back into port and that he wouldn't do well up there without us. I really knew that.

Charlie said that his legs were getting numb in the water, waiting. Then he harassed Sam again.

Sam just stared down at the water.

"Sam," I yelled up to him. "I've changed my mind! You're not allowed to jump! Do you get it? Not allowed."

I was worried that he'd hit his head. But I was also worried about Kit leaving us, and I projected this worry onto Sam, though I couldn't see this then.

"So we're *formally* not allowed to jump, Mom?" he yelled.

"It's formal. No jumping!"

Then he climbed down the side of the cliff and had to hold on to the roots of the wild rosebushes and anything else he could put his hands on. I almost couldn't watch. It looked scarier than jumping.

When he got to the water, he swam out to Charlie and they floated away. I devoured them with my eyes, until all I could see was the tops of their shoulders and their furred hair.

ON THE WAY HOME, none of us mentioned how Sam hadn't jumped. He was still in the habit of letting himself feel inferior, and it was better not to say anything.

We played Scrabble at the table by the window after dinner, and Kit spelled *ass*.

The word was too easy, and I thought the boys would never fall for it.

But they almost convulsed, they laughed so hard. They could not get over how funny Kit was.

He told them that he'd miss them while he was gone.

I'd asked him earlier to say this. He was going to be away so long.

Then he pounded on his chest, as if that would do the rest of the talking for him.

Later, after the boys had climbed up to the loft, Kit and I stood by the window and looked at the shape of the trawler in the dark. It was the first time he was going to leave his boat and fish off someone else's. I think he was trying to see it as anything but a defeat.

He put his arm around me and said he was going to Canada just this once, so he never had to leave the *Jillian Lynne* again.

I saw how hopeful he was. This is what I chose to call it. And that if he lost the trawler, it would be such a dispossession he might never recover.

"You can't not come see me," he said. "I won't make it if you don't come."

We kissed once, and I felt the warmth start in my stomach and move between my legs. I leaned in to him and kissed him harder and was hungry for him then.

He took a step back and said, "I'm not sure how I'm going to do it."

I had my hand on his shoulder. "Do what, Kit?"

"Leave for three months."

I looked at his face in the light, and his ruddy skin, and angular cheekbones that tapered down to his jaw, and the hair wavier and wilder from swimming.

He kissed me again and put his hand inside my jeans to the place he always found there.

I think I moaned a little. Then I laughed. I don't know why really.

"What?" He looked at me.

He always took our sex seriously, maybe even more that night because he was leaving. I think he was nervous and sad. But he couldn't say this. He was not the kind of person who could confide in anyone, really. Or maybe our sex was how he confided.

"Nothing." I smiled.

Maybe I'd laughed because I couldn't get my mind around the three months either. It seemed impossible. I knew he needed to go, but that I'd resent him for leaving. I already did and he hadn't left yet.

I took his hand and led him to our bed and sat him down and pulled his jeans off. I took off his T-shirt and kissed his stomach and his neck and his mouth.

Then I took all my clothes off.

He watched me the whole time, and I smiled but didn't let myself laugh.

I sat on top of him then, and he put his arms around me and we moved together. I came slowly at first. Then we moved faster. Afterward, he pulled me down on the bed next to him and we held hands, and it felt like something so good had been sealed between us. Neither of us said anything about him leaving. We were tired, and he only had a few hours to sleep before he had to go.

HE BECAME MORE HIMSELF after the surgery but also sadder in the hospital. His blood pressure fluctuated, and there were hours of silence and moods.

After the first week, Linda made me go to the Halifax Best Western for one night, even though I didn't want to.

She said my exhaustion was catching up with me and that Kit needed me rested, and she knew I wasn't really sleeping in the chair by his bed.

So I left the hospital and went to the hotel, and it wasn't good and I didn't sleep at all. I worried about the boys and if they were okay without me, and I worried about Kit and if he was in too much pain and had no one in the room to help him.

I drove back to the hospital in the morning and sat in the chair by his bed again, and I think he liked it. That I was there.

He kept saying he wanted to go home.

The bifocal surgeon came in the afternoon and told us the rehabilitation would take at least another week, and that then they would decide if they'd let him do the rest of the rehab in Maine. But it could be months, the surgeon told us, before Kit was really walking again.

I remember Kit asked me things about my film after the surgeon left, and if I had enough footage and whether I was pleased with it. I was happy that he asked. It was a good sign, even if he was just pretending to be interested.

I told him that I had hours and hours of his people talking

and laughing and working in the village, and that his past had become my preoccupation while he'd been gone and that I needed to distill it down to sixty minutes. I said sixty minutes could be the most consequential hour of your life. Or the whirring of 3,600 faceless seconds. We've gotten so good at erasing time with mindless technology.

I heard a dog bark in the hall then, and this was surprising. I hadn't heard an animal the whole time I'd been in the hospital.

Then a woman opened the door and peered in.

She had long, black, wavy hair, feathered in front, and a serious face. And when she shoved the door all the way open with her shoulder, my first thought was, Here we go again. Another of Kit's followers.

She had a black duffel bag in her right hand that was only partly zipped, so you could see the top half of a little dog in the bag, maybe some kind of terrier. She put the bag on the floor and took the dog out and held it up to her face and told it to be quiet. "Or we'll get kicked out of here, Maxwell."

Then she waved at me and said her name was Marsh.

Kit said, "Jill, please meet the woman who called the Coast Guard after the boat caught on fire." He didn't look at me while he talked. He looked at her, so it was the strangest feeling.

Marsh said she'd been a fish cutter on the boat and the cook, and that Kit had chosen the dog for her at the shelter, so she was forever grateful to him.

She talked very loudly.

I wanted her to leave. We'd been quiet in the room for days.

I got up from the chair and stood by the bathroom door and stared at the tattoo on her right wrist. Three intricate black roses all woven together. I couldn't believe the time the tattoo must have required.

Kit smiled at her. "Don't pretend you hadn't been thinking on a dog just like him."

I thought I'd suffocate when he smiled at her. I almost could not breathe. I could tell she looked up to him, but that he also got something from her.

She kissed the dog's little head. "After Kit pointed him out to me, I was a goner."

I think I said something about how Kit was a dog whisperer in another life. But what I was really thinking was that they needed to stop flirting. I wouldn't be able to breathe again until they stopped.

Charlie called on my cell phone then, and my heart leapt.

"How's Dad?" he said.

"He's okay today. He's pretty good." But my heart was loud in my ears because of the woman with the dog and the way Kit kept smiling at her.

I walked out into the hallway, where the connection was better. "Can you hear me, Charlie? It's still going to take some time before Dad can really walk." I leaned my head back against the cinder blocks. "But tell me you're okay?"

"Well, there's no privacy here, and Sam keeps trying to hurt me."

Charlie had started demanding more privacy after he'd met Lucy, and I understood it. But he and Sam were also wrestling more, so it was confusing. It seemed like Charlie was regressing, but I didn't know you could move forward and backward when you were a teenager, almost simultaneously.

When they wrestle, Sam's more like Kit. Deeply into it and almost taking pleasure in the pain. Sometimes it seems like Sam's getting his vengeance for being the second born.

Charlie isn't a natural fighter. I think he's more like me. But he wants the physical contact, and he likes solving problems with his body. I can't stop the boys from wrestling. I try. But sometimes it gets almost violent and then it's scary. I think the boys feel it too, and that it has had to do with Kit not being in the house with us.

I hadn't wanted to leave the boys at Jimmy's. I knew Jimmy wouldn't stop the wrestling. He might even think it was a good thing. But Candy was down in Wells helping her daughter Lisa with her new baby, and my mother, who still lives up in Harwich, couldn't come because she's on an oxygen machine. The boys would undo her with their energy without her even knowing it.

Sam got on the phone then and told me Charlie was *lying* and hurting *him*.

I knew Sam was suffering, but I can't always tell if it's a big suffering with him or a small suffering. The only way for me to really know was to go home.

"*When* are you guys coming back?" he said.

I told him that it would just be me. There was no way Dad could come.

"Please just come home. I really think you should come."

I walked back into Kit's room, and the clock on the wall above his IV pole said 10 a.m. It takes seven hours to get to Sewall from the hospital on a good day. Kit put his hand out to pet the dog, and Marsh moved closer to the bed so Kit could reach the dog's head.

I felt like I was losing the boys then. It was a feeling inside my body that they needed me then more than Kit did. Why I thought the boys needed me more, I still don't understand. But Sam had asked me to come, and this was not like him. I thought if Kit really needed me, he would have said.

I sat down in the green chair and packed up my laptop and books and took the few clothes I'd brought and put them in my canvas bag.

Marsh stood by the bed with the dog in her arms, and Kit talked to the dog and told him that he was a good boy and he'd see him again soon.

I couldn't leave until Marsh left. That was one rule I made for myself. The other rule was to make sure that after I was gone, Kit would think of our time together in the hospital as a kind time. A time without recrimination. He'd been my great love for so long.

I went into the bathroom and gathered my things in there and when I came out, Marsh had put the dog back in the bag and was standing by Kit's bed again. They were both quiet, and she was watching him scratch the top of the dog's head.

He looked like he was doing it without thinking, and I felt a little crushed by this but there was nothing really to point to.

Then Marsh said, "Maxwell and I are out of here," and she smiled this smile at me. It was the conspiratorial smile between women that I've never understood. Like we're in on a joke. But I didn't know what the joke was.

After she left, Kit looked at me. "Do you like her?"

I thought the Dilaudid must have been working well, because he seemed much younger to me then and not like himself.

"She has a really sweet dog." It was all I could think of to say.

"The best," he said.

Then I told him that I had to go.

"Go where?"

"We have children, Kit. Remember them? I've got to go home."

"Not today. No way. I can't imagine it here without you."

"Something's off at your dad's. They're wrestling too much. One of them's going to get hurt."

He closed his eyes. "They're playing you. You know that, right? They're fine."

I put my hand on his forehead and studied the creases around his eyes and the age lines down the sides of his face. This face in the hospital was a different face but still the face I loved. Softer now. The jaw less prominent somehow.

I think I was angry about Marsh and the dog, and I couldn't sort it out. I didn't know what it meant or why she'd come. But I would have stayed if he'd asked me again.

I leaned down and kissed his lips.

"Mmmm," he said. "More, please."

I stayed with him thirty more minutes or so, holding his hand and talking. But if I'm honest, the whole time I stood there, I kept thinking about the boys and when I could get in my car and leave.

I GOT TO JIMMY'S around five-thirty on that Saturday, and the boys were basically high from a computer shooting game called Halo. I knew they'd stopped playing right before I walked in because of how sweaty and dazed they looked on the couch.

Jimmy told me that he'd tried to get them to stop and go outside, but they wouldn't listen. Then he shook his head and went back into the kitchen, where he was frying a steak.

All the euphoria I'd had on the drive down about rescuing the boys evaporated. Sam acted offended when we got in the car and I told him the video game did things to his brain.

He yelled that I was wrong and that I always assumed things about him.

Charlie said I was way off. "You have no right to come back and accuse us of things, Mom. No right at all."

We drove in silence after that. Kit's accident had already made us meaner. I didn't know what would become of us. We took *The Duchess* to the island, and I cooked them pasta and went to bed.

When I woke up in the morning, my thoughts were less dramatic. The trees outside the windows dripped with water, which meant it had rained while I was sleeping, and there was a thick fog so everything looked unearthly. I put my raincoat on and went down to check the boats. The water was a dark slate color, and calm. More like a lake than an ocean. The fog was thickest by the shoreline, and I could move my hand through it like I was slicing weighted air. I started thinking about the woman with the dog in the hospital. Then I thought I was making things up.

When I went back inside, Charlie asked me where Kit's boots were. I pointed to the metal bin next to the door. Then I drank my second coffee at the table.

Sam climbed down the ladder in his boxers. Charlie was already on the float, bailing *The Duchess* in Kit's boots, and I knew Sam would be mad about the boots. Sam wants almost anything Charlie has, and I think this is partly birth order and also just their personalities.

Sam ate his eggs cold and said he wanted to be wearing something of Kit's, like Charlie was.

I said this was a great idea and that he could go into Kit's closet and find anything he wanted.

This is how I appeased Sam without his knowing. They can never know.

He came out of the bedroom in an old wool vest I'd forgotten Kit had.

I told Sam that Kit was going to be okay.

He nodded at me like he believed me and needed to believe me. He looked so young.

I stood up from the table and went to him, and he let me hug him. This was why I'd come home.

*PART TWO*

**SAY VERY LITTLE**

I CLIMB OUT OF bed now and stir the coals in the woodstove and put two logs in. Who would be so stupid as to put a picture of themselves smoking pot on Instagram? The sun rises above the trees and fills our little house with light. When I call up to the boys, their names condense in the cold.

It's dangerous to talk to Sam about punishment before he's had calories. You never know how he'll react. I wait until he's eating his oatmeal at the table by the windows before I tell him I'm taking his phone away.

"Why," he says, "would you ever, ever do that?" He looks at me for a moment like he's really afraid.

"Because of your Instagram crime that will go henceforth unmentioned until after school, but of which I'm sure you're aware."

"Please stop talking so weirdly. It's not what you think. It's not."

"Cameras don't lie, Sam."

I reach for his phone by the stove, because what else can I do?

"Stupid move, Sam. What were you thinking?" I don't know if I'm angrier about the pot or the photo. "Oh, and you're grounded this week."

"Mom, that word's like from another century. What does it even mean?"

"It means come home right after school and no going to Robbie's house for band practice."

He pushes the chair back and stands. "How long are you going to keep the phone? How long? Until infinity?"

"Probably infinity." I take a long sip of coffee by the sink. My hands are shaking. "I'm keeping the phone a week, but really, Sam? That's all you have to say? How about *sorry*?"

"Please don't take it. It's my *life*. Why do you obsess over it, Mom? It's like you're obsessed."

"I don't obsess." I put the phone by my heart. "I parent. This is called parenting."

It's good that he's mad. But he rattles me, and I try not to show it. I walk into my bedroom with the peeling windowsills and hide his phone in my underwear drawer like it's a small handgun.

Sometimes the line between empathy and consequences gets so blurred with him that I can't see it. When to press and when to let up. I want to go back to the way we were before Liam died, as if we were only ever happy then.

"You know what?" I walk into the kitchen. "I had ambition in art school, so even though I didn't have money, I was okay. Don't give up on yourself, Sam. Don't stop being ambitious."

He fakes a smile at me. "Once again I have absolutely *no idea* what you're talking about, Mom."

"Just say, 'Okay, Mom,'" Charlie coaches him. "Just say, 'Yes, Mom. Whatever you say, Mom.'"

Sam stands and salutes me. "Yes, Mom. Yes, *sir*!"

I laugh and go put my arms around his shoulders.

He screams like I'm physically hurting him.

Then he tries another tactic and lectures me on the merits of edible marijuana. Will I buy him some?

He wants me to laugh, because I always forgive him when he makes me laugh.

"Edibles?" I'm trying to do something with my hair in the mirror by the door. I recently dyed it a burned black color, and it now sits on my head in the shape of a helmet. "Have you completely lost your mind?"

I turn and stare at the channel between our island and the mainland, looking for signs of whales. The water is a rich gray, and it ripples and swirls like the thickest silk. It's cold water. But the air is colder and robin's-egg blue, and you can see for miles on the straight horizon line. There are rarely whales, but I like thinking about them and other prehistoric things that live in the ocean. This gives me comfort. Kit's trawler pulls on its mooring ball in the channel like a large chained animal, and this doesn't give me comfort.

I finally train my gaze on Sam. He's something elemental to me, like good bread or water. But someone needs to save me from him.

"She'll *never* do edibles," Charlie says with his mouth full of oatmeal. Then he slides to the fridge in his white tube socks, takes out the OJ, and slides back. "Don't you understand she's a big no on drugs?"

"See." I point to Charlie, who looks much older in Kit's red flannel shirt. "I'll never do it."

Sam gets up to pee and the whole little house creaks. There are sixteen pine planks from floor to roof, which have darkened and swollen over time. Sam hardly ever closes the bathroom door all the way. I can hear the torrent of pee and am sure he got it all over the seat.

What can be so incredibly difficult about putting the seat up? If I had to count the times I've sat in his cold pee I'd be a sad, bitter woman.

"Dad will be home in a couple weeks," I call to him. It's the Canadian doctor's best guess on Kit's recovery.

"*Weeks?*" Sam comes and leans on the counter. His khakis are rolled to look retro, but really they're just too short.

"Don't forget we're driving up there on Friday," I say. "That's in four days, Sam. Count them. Four."

He doesn't say anything.

Maybe he hasn't heard me.

Then he says, "*Really,* Mom? *Weeks?* Who are these doctors, anyway? Dad's already been gone the whole f—ing fall."

Charlie brings his oatmeal bowl to the sink and says, "That was commendable, Sam, not to swear."

KIT BROUGHT ME TO the island for the first time in his old dayboat with the black steering wheel. This was in August of 1997, and I was a waitress at the lodge on the mainland where he delivered lobsters and became the boy most of the waitresses wanted to sleep with. Think *Dirty Dancing* without the Catskills. Our boss was a former high school wrestling champion who called me Pretty Girl several times a day. Hey, Pretty Girl, why aren't you smiling?

I was smiling. Just not at him. But even he couldn't stop me from loving that job.

Our waitress uniform was a royal-blue polyester dress that zipped up the front, and in the mornings we had to turn the industrial coffee machine on and pour water in. Except one morning near the end of that summer, I forgot to put the water in. When the burning smell made it out to the dining room, several guests asked me what we were incinerating in the kitchen.

My boss found me next to the walk-in freezer, getting more ice for the water pitchers, and he was so angry about the coffee machine situation that he grabbed my arm and tried to twist it.

I ran out to the porch, where Kit was unloading lobsters from his flatbed. He stopped and walked over to me, and we stood together looking out over the rusted dumpsters.

"What's his name?" he said.

"Whose name?"

"The guy who made you cry?" He had excited blue eyes, and wavy hair, and an ease about him. Like no calamity was too big.

I dried my eyes and smiled. "Why do you think there's been any crying?"

He laughed at me then and his eyes crinkled in the sun, and that was pretty much it for me.

FIVE DAYS LATER HE took me to the island in his boat and pointed to the little house on the ledge and said he planned to live there someday. Then he steered us over to the tip of the spear and took his T-shirt off and handed it to me. I climbed out the bow with my camera around my neck and his shirt in my hand, while he anchored and swam in. It was one of the last truly hot days of summer, and he put the shirt back on and we made our way up the ledge together, holding hands on the steepest part.

It was the first time we'd really touched, and I couldn't believe it was finally happening. I think I said something silly, like "God, I love islands."

He said, "But I didn't think you were a romantic."

I thought it was sexy, how he believed he had some deeper knowledge of me.

He pointed to the moon then, which was starting to rise over the horizon. I thought this was romantic of *him,* and I wondered if he was playing with me. I couldn't tell yet if he was the kind of person who really trusted anyone.

We walked through the forest in the middle of the island, and I took photos, but what I really wanted to do was kiss him. I was leaving in the morning because the summer season was over, and everything on the island was hypnotic with meaning, if you were me and wanted it to be.

At the southern end the ledge was high and steep, and he said we could pretend to see all the way across the ocean to France. He took my hand again, and my heart made the loud, pounding sound.

The afternoon had the yellow, glassy light that we get in late August in Maine, and the heat felt loose around my body so it was still possible to pretend summer wouldn't be overshadowed by fall. I let my arm brush against his and was glad for his taut stomach above his narrow hips and for the fact of his body.

We sidestepped down the rocks, hand in hand, until we came to the little beach. I'd been to a beach almost every day that summer with the other waitresses, and we'd shared our Coppertone. Kit said we had to jump the final part down to the sand. When we landed, we kissed, and his mouth was warm and perfect.

He pulled me down on top of him in the sand, and we kissed again, harder this time. He moved his hands over my T-shirt, first across my breasts and then down the sides of my ribcage. My body felt almost new to me, and there was this vast happiness.

Later, we lay on our backs looking up at the sky, and he said, "A storm is coming tomorrow, while you're on the road."

"How do you know that?" I leaned over and kissed him again. "How can you tell?"

"The wind's shifted south to north. You'll be gone. It will rain, and I'll never see you again."

He wasn't usually dramatic. So maybe we really would never see each other again. But this didn't seem possible.

I said, "What do you care?" But I knew he could detect my fakeness, and that I didn't need to try so hard around him, the way I did at school when I pretended I wasn't from a part of Maine no one had heard of.

"I care." He sat up and took my hand and appeared to be studying it. He was so focused on this part of me that it allowed me to become more myself, if that was possible.

He was deciding about me then, while the waves poured over the seaweed, and I didn't think that in the end he would be able to accept me. It had to do with class, though this wasn't really accurate, because neither of us was from money. It had more to do with fishing, which was its own status in Maine and wasn't about class but something bigger, tied to the past and the ocean and survival.

He told me then that the island was in his blood and that fishing was all his family knew, so it was his destiny. I think he really believed this. I didn't know anyone else who talked like this.

I already knew I'd leave Maine. I didn't know how or when, but it was my destiny in a way. In Maine you were either staying or going. Both required their own set of skills and risks, and you had to choose.

The ocean looked almost aquamarine, and the trees were bright from all the rain, so the island had a strip of green running through the middle. I told myself I'd never forget the island or the kissing. No matter where I went or what I did. But some part of me was also trying to win Kit's heart so that I could keep it. I really wanted to keep it.

OUR DOCK SITS IN a tiny cove near the point of the spear, protected from currents and tides by the rock ledges. To get down to it we have to take the wooden ramp Kit built over the rocks and go past the wild rosebushes and sumac and cedar scrub.

*The Duchess* won't start again today. But Sam keeps pulling on the engine rope until I'm sure he's flooded it.

"I live in a police state," he says. "The way you're always watching me. That should be illegal, Mom. For you to go on my Instagram."

I'm up in the bow, where I want to remind him not to flood the engine again and that years ago he let me "follow" him on Instagram. But I stop myself from saying anything.

We had another killing frost last night. But the potatoes are all dug now, and the gardens are covered with seaweed. I'm not afraid of the cold. If anything, I'm afraid of Sam, because he isn't in control of himself anymore now that his father's gone.

Your dad almost died. This is what I told the boys when I first explained the accident to them. Your father almost died in the boat fire. I told them this because it's true, and also so that the boys would remember to be nicer to me. I don't really mean that. I told them so they could understand how serious things were.

I read an article in Kit's hospital room last week about a painter in Los Angeles named Laura Owens who had a retrospective at the Whitney in New York at the age of forty-seven. My mother always told me the whole world was waiting for me, and in this way I was not one of the girls whose appetite was taken away. But who gets a Whitney retrospective at forty-seven?

The question for me is how to survive on the island with the boys and remain *chill*. The question blows up almost every day. Candy says you wait it out and the boys come back to you. She says it can take maybe five years. I don't know if I can wait that long.

Laura Owens kept a journal in her twenties called "How to Be the Greatest Artist in the World," with a fourteen-point checklist with things like "Think Big" on it. And "Do Not Be Afraid of Anything." And "Say Very Little." I've decided to try to implement the say-very-little concept as a new communication strategy. My hope is that by withholding, I'll receive signs that my little boys are in there behind the faces of the impostors.

"Shit." Sam kicks the black casing of the Evinrude, then kicks the side of the boat.

"Please don't do that." My mind is stuck on *thinly rolled joint, thinly rolled joint. Joint thinly rolled.*

"Don't do what?" He kicks the side of the boat again and looks at me.

"Swear." But what I really mean is, Don't kick the boat.

Even that's not true. What I want to say is, Don't seal yourself off in your pain. And, Don't smoke joints in cars outside McDonald's. And, Don't die. And, Where are you these days? Where are you?

The ocean is a mysterious plum color with engravings like the back of a nickel.

"Please don't swear and don't kick the boat." I try to speak with as little emotion as possible in hopes of neutralizing him. "If you do it again, we're getting out and no one's going to school."

I'm not used to giving orders and am vaguely embarrassed that my strategy until recently has involved being more like their friend. But now that Kit's gone, it comes down to how to recognize opportunities with the boys and convert.

When Sam and Charlie were younger, they called themselves the smoking police and decreed that Kit couldn't smoke in the house anymore. It was a blow. He liked to come home from fishing trips and smoke and stare out the window at the trawler. It seemed back then that we might have caught all the fish there were to catch in the Gulf of Maine.

Then the government organized the Maine fleet into something called sectors, which are cooperatives with an allocation system of how much fish you can catch, based on numbers of fish you landed the ten years before 2006. Kit didn't have great numbers for his landings. The groundfish in the Gulf of Maine had pretty much dried up then, and the *Jillian Lynne* is only forty-feet long—not big enough to go farther out to sea. The math on his quota punished him, and he had terrible allocation.

He patched it together by shrimping in the winter, but six years ago they shut down the shrimp fishery. Haddock and flounder have started to come back now, and many fishermen say there are more cod. But Kit doesn't have good quota, and the prices at auction in Portland leave him almost in the negative. Plus it all just keeps consolidating. More regulation and more corporations from away buying up boats and permits. Maine isn't an industrial fishery. At least not yet. Local people own the fleet. They're just trying to make a living.

THE WIND PUSHES SAM'S hair up and puffs out the sides of his sweatshirt. He looks like a lunatic. Why won't he wear a coat? What's wrong with a coat?

"Sam." Charlie's losing patience. "I'll kill you if you make me late for school."

Then Charlie stands, and the boat starts to rock. His cargo pants have the ratted-out pockets, and he's got the patched black parka on, and Kit's Patriots hat. The hat pangs me. Kit always wore the hat.

For a second I'm pretty certain we're going to tip. But then Charlie lands in the stern, and Sam's in the middle seat, and the boat rights itself.

"Please," Sam says. "Please consider edibles, Mom."

"I thought we covered edibles at breakfast?" I look across to the mainland, which is all green forest, except for a handful of summer cottages.

I know Sam wishes Kit and I could switch places, so I'm in the hospital and Kit's on the boat. I've read about this phase where the boy needs the father more and lets the mother go. Part of me is honestly ready to be let go of, because I'm not as good as Kit is at saving Sam from himself.

Sometimes I think he's confusing his grief over Liam with his grief for Kit. Kit will be back, I keep telling Sam. Your father will come home. Why can't he see that?

. . .

ONCE UPON A TIME there were seven trawlers in the channel, but that was back during the cod era and the better prices.

Now there's just Kit's boat. And we are in what he calls the
post-cod era. My hope today is to get a loan extension on the trawler
from the credit union officer. A man who was in Kit's tenth-grade
biology class.

Charlie pushes the choke and pulls on the engine rope, which
revs high because of the extra gas in the line. I've got on the dark
skinny jeans still somewhat in fashion, and the down coat that
makes me look like an amoeba. I tell Charlie please not to get me
wet.

Sam says, "Edibles are good for muscle pain, Mom. They're
good for stress."

"Since when is playing preseason basketball and going to
Dunkin' Donuts stressful, Sam?" Charlie is standing in the stern,
steering. "Do you know I haven't even gotten high yet, Sam? I
haven't even gotten drunk? That's *insane* at my age!"

"Please don't pretend you're Dad, Charlie," Sam says.

"You have to stop scolding him." I look hard at Charlie, because
this is something we're working on—how he tries to parent Sam
while Kit's gone. It's not good for any of us. He's usually more
patient. We all are with Sam. We root for him and hold Sam up.

Kit says I do this too much. Hold Sam up. We've argued about
this, Kit and I, more than anything else except money. Because I'll
always hold Sam up.

"Lara would let me try edibles," Sam says.

Lara is my friend who paints beautiful, moody oil paintings
and says if she ever catches me wearing mom jeans she'll airlift me
from the island. She's now the professor of visual arts at the college

we went to together in Portland. A place my father once called the $15,000 bachelor of fine arts degree in weaving. Even though I never took weaving and was on full scholarship.

"Lara would understand me."

"Oh really." I look up at the sky. Please, someone help me.

WE CLIMB OUT OF *The Duchess* and take the dirt path up to the trees. There's sap on the windshield again, but no one seems to care but me. We're a one-Subaru family. Both boys have their licenses now, but Sam's in the restricted period when he can't have anyone in the car with him except immediate family.

"You know what I've realized, Mom?" Charlie says from the passenger seat.

"No, what?" I'm pawing in my bag for the keys.

"You never go out."

"Out where?"

"You never leave the house at night."

The car still smells like the dead mouse in the exhaust pipe last week.

"Where do you want me to go?"

"I need you to go out. I need you to go get dinner with Lara."

Half of Sam's McMuffin from yesterday is on the floor by the gas pedal. I nudge it back with my clog until it's mostly under my seat.

"Lara lives in Portland. That's almost two hours away. I can't just go there for dinner. I'm being a mother, in case you didn't notice."

"Oh, we noticed." Sam puts in his earphones and leans his head back on the seat.

"I need you to please go out this week," Charlie says. "So Lucy and I can cook."

It's freezing in the car. I crank the heat. "So you can cook what?"

"I don't know. Cook anything. We're never really alone."

I drive through the pine trees where the baby foxes live and think about my bedroom and how it's such a nice bedroom with the view of the glassy water and the big tin sky. I don't want Charlie to have sex in my bedroom, but I don't want to insult him by implying that he *would* have sex in my bedroom. Still, where else would he have sex in the house?

We're on the tar road now, and I want to formulate my strategy for Sam's joint on Instagram, not a strategy for how not to let Charlie have sex in my bedroom.

"I'll leave the house, and you can have Lucy over."

Did I just really say that? What would Kit say?

"But wait," I say. "What about your brother?"

"Sam can stay at Robbie's."

"So you can have sex with Lucy in the house?"

"*Mom.*" Charlie does not turn to look at me. "What are you *saying?*"

I've read that it's important to talk to your teenage boys about sex. And that while the girls are having urgent conversations about pleasure and consent, the boys are having zero conversations. The boys are alone, and apparently want these conversations but don't know how to initiate them.

Kit says that Jimmy never spoke a word to him about sex, and he turned out okay, didn't he?

Still, who really wants to be on their own with this stuff if they don't have to be?

But then I chicken out and don't tell Charlie about the condoms I found in his room last week. It was a box of ten and there were only five condoms left. I was looking for the stapler he keeps in his desk. The condoms looked like a box of Band-Aids. Until then I hadn't ever considered the idea of Charlie having sex. I'm still not close to over it. I put the box back where I found it and walked out of the room as if I were leaving a crime scene.

"What will you make?" I turn the radio on. It helps to have Hall and Oates in the car with me.

"Make *when*?" Charlie says.

"What will you make for dinner with Lucy?"

Charlie is here in the car with us but his mind is with Lucy. He's crossed over some imaginary river with her and left Sam and me on the other side. This is confusing to all of us, in the way that no one understands exactly what's happening when love strikes someone down.

"I don't *know*, Mom." He sounds irritated now, as if having Lucy for dinner were my idea in the first place.

It is amazing how the conversation becomes an indictment of me when I wasn't the one who started it. This happens to me all the time.

"But isn't that the goal?"

"Of what?"

"Of having dinner with Lucy? To make something to eat?"

"We'll cook steak, maybe. Or pasta. We just want to be alone for once." He looks out the window and sighs. Weight of the world on his shoulders.

"Isn't that the reason we don't leave you alone?"

"What are you talking about now?"

I take one hand off the steering wheel and put it on his shoulder and try to connect. "Honey, isn't the reason parents don't leave their teenagers alone in their houses on Friday nights because you're going to have sex if we leave you alone, and we're not supposed to want you to have sex?"

I regret it as soon as I've said it, but I can't take it back. This is the thing with wolves. How many times they've made me want to take things back.

"Mom, I can't believe you. I can't. You're just so *wrong*."

He puts his hands over his face and turns toward Sam, who's fast asleep or in a music coma. "I'm not talking to you anymore, Mom. I'm not speaking to you. It's like I'm not here now."

I pull up to the curb in front of the high school, and both boys jump out. The building looks like an imposing bank from the 1950s, and Charlie starts run-walking toward it. He hates to be late.

It's unclear if Sam is planning on ever going inside. He sees some friends over on the stone wall by the flagpole and sits down between them.

I should get out of the car and ask him whether he intends to attend class today. But part of me is tired of confronting him. Maybe he can be the school's problem for a little while.

TED CRAWFORD'S OFFICE IS a cramped white cubicle at the back of the Avery Credit Union. He is a pensive man on a good day and wears the kind of glasses that change color based on the amount of light in the room. The glasses are gray today, which makes him look more tired than usual, and I'd be tired too if I had to tell the fishermen I grew up with that I can't pull them back from the brink. But Ted's one of the good guys. He's helped Kit and me out more than most would.

The credit union is downtown in the old brick pharmacy. Everything in this part of Avery looks up at the bridge. It's been two years since Liam drowned, but I'm sitting in Ted's cubicle staring out the one window, and I swear I can see Sam and Liam up on the bridge in their full catastrophe. Then I have to get a grip on myself. Why does everything on days like this still seem so desperate?

Ted tells me that although he would like to be able to help us, he's sorry to report that in the end he can't support another line of credit on the *Jillian Lynne*.

It's taken me years not to feel embarrassed that Kit named the trawler after me. It is the custom here. And if on one level it's flattering to have a boat named after you, it's also a strange thing. I've had to stop myself from assuming that when someone like Ted talks about the boat, he isn't really talking about me.

He says he heard about Kit's injury, and he wants me to know that everyone in Avery is cheering for him.

"Thank you," I say. "Really, thank you."

But what I want to tell him is that cheering doesn't matter and I don't see how we can get out of this mess. At one time they might have caught all the fish there were to catch, but they know some things now about how to rebound a species, and Kit just needs a little help with the boat payments.

Ted says that he could probably do more for us if I got a regular job. "Something with steady hours, Jill." He lays his hands out flat on his desk. "You know, where you file a standard W-2 and we see consistency."

I tell him that I've got a job, and that the grants for my film came in right on time this year. Three of the state museums funded me, and the Humanities Council, and even the NEA. But Ted doesn't know how on the drive in this morning I thought hard about applying for a job at L.L. Bean. They're hiring for the winter season. It would be a long commute but good, reliable money.

I MAKE MY WAY out of the credit union and climb in the Subaru on Front Street and close my eyes and breathe. I'm going down to the village to film Shorty Kater. He's been deciding all fall whether or not to sell his fishing pier to a developer from New Jersey, and he has news for me today.

Shorty is the son of Jimmy's younger sister. If you say *Sewall village* around here, people know you mean Archers and you mean Jimmy. He's got one of the biggest lobster boats on the coast and owns the lobster pound, and in this way he's like a village king in Ireland. Everyone needs his blessing to do just about anything.

At first Jimmy didn't want me talking to anyone for my film. He didn't understand how a film was going to help save his village. He doesn't go to films. Or only if they have Clint Eastwood in them.

I told him that you can lose only so much of your heritage before there's no going back. I said we needed to protect the waterfront and that the film would help. It was our responsibility. I told him there were only twenty commercial fishing boats left in the state and twenty miles of working waterfront.

Maine's a big place, I said then. Twenty miles. Twenty boats in the fleet. That's it. Which is when I think I got him.

He's a proud man and proudest of his village. I know he doesn't want it to change into something it was never intended to be.

WHEN YOU COME UPON the village in a car, you're looking down on it from the top of the hill, and it appears enchanted like in a children's book with drawings of the place where fisherpeople live—fifty or so little wooden houses with dark green forest on three sides and a picturesque harbor at the bottom. People come from hundreds of miles away and from other countries to photograph it.

Candy's store is in a clapboard house on the ledge above the harbor. She and Flip raised their three kids here. It's a general store that sells milk and batteries and bologna and ice cream. In the mornings before the sun's up, Candy makes eggs and pots of coffee for the fishermen and serves them at a counter in the back.

Flip's icehouse is next to the store. A flat-roofed steel box where fishermen and lobstermen and oyster farmers and clammers and seaweed harvesters get their ice. Jimmy's wharf sits beside the icehouse, and the pound is inside a wooden shed at the end of the wharf, where the boats tie up to unload.

Everyone knows everyone in the village. This isn't meant to sound sentimental. Everyone knows where you're going in your boat, and how your daughter did in the middle-school play, and if your marriage is off the rails. And anyone who's not in some way related to someone in the village is a little suspect. I went to art school and make documentary films and wear clogs in winter, so I've never fully gotten over my outsider status.

Sometimes I think I'm shooting this film in the village to show that I belong here. When I'm actually making the film, I'm completely sure about what I'm doing. It's only later that I wonder.

I EMBED IN A town and shoot everyone and every-
thing. There's nothing planned about it, really. The films become
a conversation that often ends up talking about the purpose work
gives people in Maine.

I've made a film about the mill town I grew up in. And one
about the shoe factories in Lewiston. And the shipyard in Bath.

My films are not nostalgic. At least I try not to let them be.
They don't hold on to the past. I think they explore the idea of
change and whether change has to mean suffering to people.

The first film I made features my father. In the opening scene
he stands outside the mill in his one dark suit and military hair
and looks like a handsome, earnest undertaker. He says the mill
is empty now, except for the kids who smoke *the marijuana* and
climb inside with their skateboards through the broken windows
that line the western wall, along the parking lot.

In another scene my father says that he keeps hearing about
all the new money coming into the state, but he and my mother
don't see it. This scene is shot at my parents' farmhouse. The one
I grew up in. You can hear my mother say *Where is it?* referring
to the money. Then you hear her laugh and cough her gravelly
smoker's cough. The camera pans to her in the TV room, sitting
in her plaid recliner by the window, knitting another afghan and
breathing on her oxygen machine.

My mother used to sew clothes for people. Once a year she let
my sister, Sasha, and me choose a back-to-school outfit at Sears.

My mother loved Sears. She'd hold clothes up to her body in the dressing room mirror, but she never bought herself anything.

I have a sense that my mother was trapped in our town, but I don't have clear evidence. It's just a feeling, because I've sometimes felt trapped on our island. The afghan she knits in the film is the one she later sent to Sasha in Jacksonville, Florida, where Sasha runs a military catering company. I wanted to tell my mother that it's hot in Florida and Sasha wouldn't need the wool blanket. But my mother has partly constructed her own reality, and I believe she's earned it.

Harwich is a harder place now, and fewer people live there. My parents are in their eighties and rely on my father's pension and Social Security. The farmhouse is falling down around them, but they refuse to leave.

"Where on earth would we go?" my father says.

WE DID THE FIRST screening of the film in Portland, and a man found me in the lobby of the theater afterward and told me he'd recently moved to Portland because of all the good food. Then he asked where I came from. He wore a black leather jacket and had spiky gray hair that made him look like the older version of Sting.

I told him I came from Harwich.

"You're from *Harwich*?" he said. Which he would have known if he'd read the credits at the end, where I thank the people I grew up with in Harwich.

He shook his head. "It's amazing to me that you come from a town like Harwich and have made such a good film."

I said, "Neither Harwich nor I has been insulted that well in a long time."

He didn't seem to hear me. He said he and his wife had been driving around the country with their dogs for months, looking for the place to live that had the best energy. They chose Maine, he said, because it hasn't been ruined yet and it felt safe.

I wasn't sure what he meant.

"We're running out of good places in America." He ran a hand through the hair. "Montana. Ruined. Too many people. Idaho ruined too. California and Seattle. Done. But I still get the right energy in Maine. There's all the new money coming in."

I wanted to tell him that almost no one I know can pay their property taxes and that most people here are just holding on.

I'd run into Kit's high school friend Steve Marshall in Avery earlier that week. Steve's brother Scotty played football with Kit and had just been arrested for selling heroin. Steve told me that Avery was filled with heroin if you knew where to look, and that anyone who has a chance should leave.

The man in the lobby said, "I've seen some children of color coming out of the high schools around here, and it surprised me. How did they get here? By what mechanism, do you think?"

I knew he was referring to the many immigrants and refugees who've come to Maine in the last twenty years. How are they here?

"How are you here?" I said to the man. "By what mechanism?" Then I walked away.

DURING THE LAST YEAR of art school, my friend Lara and I lived together on the top floor of a little clapboard on Munjoy Hill in Portland. The house had a landline and a plastic shower/tub unit, and it was a castle to me. My bedroom looked out over the white oil tanks that lined the harbor. Portland was still a dirty, edgy city that smelled like the fish pier then. There were no condos in the East End or farm-to-table restaurants in 1977. We got jobs at an oyster bar on the pier and said that together the two of us made one good waitress.

The man who owned our apartment building lived on the second floor with his wife and two kids. He still does. They yell and slam things into walls. Lara and I used to have to lie down on the floor in the kitchen because our windows looked out on the driveway, and the man, Tom, would be out there pacing. Once I came home after a shift and he was pacing and told me that his wife thought he was having affairs with two girls who worked the cash registers at Shaw's.

When Lara heard this, she said that if marriage meant being jealous of girls at the Shaw's checkout counter, then she didn't want any part of it.


WHENEVER KIT CAME TO the apartment, we hibernated. Winter fishing was harder on his body than summer fishing, and we had no money and cooked on the small electric stove and had good sex and napped. Something evened out between us. I was less in his spell and more myself, which made everything feel better and more real.

I could never tell if he was judging my life in the city. I just knew how much I liked it when he was there.

When he was gone, Lara and I went to the wharf bars and talked about what we'd do for love and honest sex. This didn't seem like too much to ask for.

She had a rule whenever she went on a date, that if she called the landline at our apartment and let it ring once and hung up, it meant she was in trouble and someone had to come get her at the address she'd left by the phone. She was adamant about this.

She never called, and I never had to rescue her. I don't know if I could have. I was busy back then trying to save myself.

Some of the students at school asked me if my family still used an outhouse. I hadn't known this was a thing, making fun of people from Maine.


I MAJORED IN PHOTOGRAPHY. The school showed me a different way to be in the world than how I'd been raised by my parents. I'd known it was out there. This new way. But I hadn't really seen it.

I didn't care about learning when I got to school. Or only in the abstract. What I cared about was what I would be allowed to do by order of my class. Many of the kids there came from money and didn't understand the paper mill or what my father did there.

But then by chance I was given a way out. My photography teacher had a brother named William Engstrom who'd been a studio-session guitar player in Nashville, and he moved to Portland to open a mixing studio on Congress Street. I started making coffee there. They paid me minimum, and I was the only girl. But no one told me I wasn't smiling enough.

Pat Benatar came to the studio to mix her album. This was a huge thing for Portland and for the studio and for the whole state, really. Pat Benatar. William Engstrom's genius wife, Julia, recorded a thirty-minute video with her, talking about what it was like to be a woman rock star. MTV picked it up, and people went crazy for it.

It's quite something to say that Pat Benatar changed my life, but it's true.

Then Julia got Nancy Wilson from Heart to do a video when she came to the studio that spring, and MTV ran that also. The videos took off. And when the semester was over, Julia asked me to fly to London with her for two months to help shoot the Chrissie Hynde video.

No one else in my family had gone to college. Now I was going to London?

KIT DROVE ME TO the airport the day I left, and asked me not to change who I was while I was gone. This was all he said about my leaving. I couldn't tell if he wanted me to stay or go.

I was fractured about it. I wanted to be with him. But my mother had told me the world was waiting.

I kissed him and got out of the truck with my bag and didn't come home for almost a year. I ended up meeting a man while I was away, and I stayed much longer than I intended.

.　.　.

JUST BEFORE I FLEW back to Maine, I called Kit from a pay phone in London and asked if he missed me. I was having a particularly bad time.

He said he did.

I knew it was a risk for him to say this. He never talked about things like missing. He didn't do emotion that way.

Then he asked if I missed him.

I said I did. I meant it. It had been my mother's dream for me to leave, and I'd wanted it too. But now I wanted him. He was what I kept thinking about.

He said his trawler was idling at the wharf and the crew was waiting.

I hung up. This was June of 1999. I knew he was the one.


I LANDED IN PORTLAND a week later and Kit picked me up in his truck. Jimmy was out lobstering when we got to the A-frame, and we went upstairs to Kit's room, and he lit a cigarette and lay on his back on one of the twin beds and said, "You seem to think that you can just come home like this." Then he closed his eyes.

It was hard for me not to lean over and kiss him, but I knew he wasn't ready to let me do that yet.

"What," he said, "did you think I'd do all that time?"

I didn't know that he was deciding to leave the woman in Avery he'd begun sleeping with. He only told me this later.

I hadn't expected to have to win him back. Though why I didn't expect this is beyond me. I sat beside him on the edge of the bed.

I said I'd loved him the whole time I'd been away. It was the truth. I knew if he let me back in, I'd have to tell him the rest of the truth later.

He said he was moving to the island and did I want to go with him?

I said I did.

I had no idea of the consequences. Or what my life would be like with him. It felt urgent and rash, but I wanted to be his family.

Then we began to undress each other.

IN THE SWEET, EARLY years on the island, the town hadn't laid underwater cable yet, and we had no electricity. We used kerosene lamps and made clearings for the gardens and built the woodpile up and fixed the house. My memory is of big rain and lightning storms that made me feel like we were shipwrecked.

We weren't worried about rising ocean levels or warming water. There were fish, and there was none of the anxiety I have now or shame that I'm not doing enough to help stop the warming.

It was like nothing I'd ever known to live in a house with a man who was physical even when he was sleeping. Everyone I knew in art school said they were going to do daring things after they graduated, and Lara and I had made a vow not to settle. The island did not feel like settling.

For Kit the island was like going home, or going deeper back into his past, I think. He liked seventies rock music and sports in that order. He took down trees and built the float and ramp and bathroom with the handheld shower contraption. He knew about tides, and the way the wind comes up from the south and hits the float, and how to fix boat engines.

I craved being around him and his salt smell. He ate on the run, grabbing slabs of cheese and meat and bread while he walked out the door. He didn't really know how to be in a house with me. A house to him was a place to walk through in a rush, drinking coffee standing up and spilling it on his way down to the float to jump in the rowboat.

Sometimes I felt like I was making something up to him. Maybe I will always be making it up to him—the fact that I once left him. When I told him about the man I'd met when I was away, I said it meant nothing to me, and he seemed to understand. Even though everyone matters in some way.

After his mother died, I think his grief was always just out of reach. She had a stroke in the kitchen of their A-frame on the mainland. It was May, and Jimmy was out lobstering, and Candy was down at the store. Kit tried to do CPR on the linoleum, but he was just a boy, and she died before the ambulance crew got there. I think he's been trying to account for what happened ever since.

No one in his family speaks of it directly. Not Jimmy or Candy or the dozen cousins. Sometimes I imagine his mother lying there while Kit tries the CPR. Kit had to live it. You would never know to look at him that he's carrying the pain. It's invisible, like most pain is.

Kit says that Jimmy didn't appear to flinch after Martha died. He threw himself into the lobster pound. But Jimmy keeps a framed photo of her in every room of the A-frame.

Candy says she raised Kit, because Jimmy was always on his boat.

KIT AND I HAVE never known money. But I've chosen to make the films, so we're a different kind of poor than the poor I was before growing up. I decided to make documentaries, because I had to. There was no other path for me, really. I took a vow to pursue the truth of people's stories, and there's not a lot of money in documentary film in Maine, but there's barely enough. I earn my expenses back and then some.

I believe in the films, and the people who come to see them

seem to believe in them. They fill the museum screenings and the festivals and theaters and grange halls where we show them.

When I'm raising money for the films, I meet people who say they had to move to Maine, like the state possessed a physical pull over them. It makes me wonder if Maine becomes some stand-in for people's lost innocence sometimes. Or if their longing for the past gets imposed onto the actual land here. Who knows. I don't begrudge anyone their longings. I have them too.

Last week I heard about three brothers from Arizona who each made millions in natural gas and bought up most of the old fishermen's houses in Pear Cove. Now the brothers want to impose a new noise ordinance. They've been seen at town meetings talking with straight faces about how they didn't come to Maine to get woken at 4 a.m. by lobster boats.

I don't know where to start with this. It's hard to get to the water in Pear Cove now because the shoreline is all privately owned. I can't think of a fisherman who has property there anymore.

SHORTY'S PIER SITS AT the mouth of the harbor, about a hundred feet south of Candy's store. Years ago Shorty put the white trailer at the end near the wooden pilings, and I set my camera up in here.

I've come with my list of questions.

Shorty puts his feet up on the metal desk littered with Marlboro boxes and Coke cans. "What in God Almighty," he says, "are we doing here?"

He and Kit are like brother-cousins, and they're the only two commercial fishermen left on the peninsula. Everyone else is in lobsters. Lobster is king now.

I get the tripod set up and extend the small boom with the microphone out over the desk. Then I plug in the light with the shade made of thick black fabric so it looks like a funnel.

"Just forget about the camera and talk to me," I tell him. "Forget the camera's even here."

He lights his first cigarette and starts bouncing his left knee.

I ask him what it means to him to be a commercial fisherman.

His face gets really serious. Then he says, "Okay, then. Okay. It's easier if you think of it like a three-legged stool, Jill."

Now he nods to himself. "You're a good, versatile fisherman. You go for groundfish in the fall, shrimp in the winter, scallops and elvers in the spring. But when the shrimp get shut down, you lose one leg of your stool. How are you going to make it without that third leg if you don't lobster and the price for your fish is lower now than it was twenty years ago?"

He puts both his hands in the air, and some of his cigarette ash falls on the desk. He says he'd lobster some if he could in the winters. And maybe Kit would too. But they never got lobster licenses when the state was basically giving them away. They didn't like lobstering. It wasn't the same as fishing. They felt like hunters when they fished, and they didn't think they'd ever need a lobster license. Now the wait is ten years.

Shorty shakes his head and takes the last drag, then puts the cigarette out in an empty Coke can. He was his father's only deckhand when he was twelve. Quit school at sixteen and became a boat captain at twenty-two. By the winter of '98 he was one of the biggest fishermen around, and then he broke his back. The accident sidelined him during some of the government's key allocation years, and his permits have such small quotas on them now.

He looks at the camera. "It comes down to price in the end. We can see the fish on the water. Last year I got $1.58 per pound. Five years ago I got $2.73. That dollar difference breaks you. You can't cover it. So many guys have quit because they couldn't make it. Have I said it's a hard life? But I'm a diehard, and there's not many of us left. Fishing is everything to me. We can't walk away. We own the boats, for Christ's sake. Though maybe I should move to Los Angeles and become a movie star after this."

He laughs at his own joke.

The developer who wants to buy his pier is planning to turn it into a marina and sell lobster rolls and onion rings.

Shorty leans so far back in the wooden chair that it looks like it's going to tip over. Then he stretches his arms out.

"I know how gentrification works," he says. "I understand it. But you can't condemn someone for trying to have a retirement, and you can't tell a fisherman what to do with his land. That is not the American way." He taps on the desk again. "When you can't make a living fishing, you begin to consider things you never thought of before, like selling."

He lights another cigarette. "I have to hand it to them down in Mass. They were better at thinking ahead than us. Maine doesn't have a big enough voice at the table. How do you take a day off to go to a fishery council *meeting* in Mass. and lose a day on the water? But how can we get bigger quotas when we don't have a seat at the table and the corporate boats are buying up all our permits?"

He frowns. "We should be an owner-operated fishery here. We live in the state. Not the corporate guys. So let me say this for your film, Miss Jillian. The Archers are a fishing family. And perhaps I'm full-on demented, because I've got so many boat repairs and I'm getting pounded by haddock coming from Iceland. But we're staying. If we sell, we're going to become a petting zoo here." He shakes his head. "Maybe we already are."

I turn the camera off and smile. Shorty and I both probably know it may just be a matter of time before something takes the village. But I can't think like that now.

He says he got Kit on the phone yesterday and Kit didn't sound good. "Strange voice or something. Only reason I called was to tell him I wasn't selling and that he should get back here and help me figure out what I'm doing with this pier."

I pack up the tripod and the camera and microphone and tell him about Sam's Instagram.

He says, "Do not ever underestimate the male capacity for recklessness. Do not ever."

"The pot is what scares the hell out of me," I say. "I think Sam loves what pot does to his brain. He has no other off switch."

Sam worked on the pier last summer. Shorty knows what makes Sam tick.

"The best thing for Sam to do is to get back on the water. Send him down to me," he says. "I've got more work here than he'll ever be able to finish."

I CALL LARA ON my way home to tell her Charlie wants to cook dinner with Lucy.

"What's wrong with that?" she says.

"Isn't that code?" I say. Mainers are good at speaking in code.

"Code for what?" Lara is the boys' godmother, which she thinks is a joke because she's basically pagan and the most undomesticated person I know.

"For sex," I say.

"What's wrong with sex?"

"There's nothing wrong with sex. It's just that it's my house and he's my son, and I haven't met her yet."

"Met who?"

"The girl my son is going to have sex with. Lucy. I thought we were meant to make it harder for them to have sex. I thought the idea was to put it off as long as we could."

"What if you die and someone asks the boys what they'll miss least about you?"

"*Least?*"

"Do you want them to say they're so relieved to finally be free of your prudishness? You need to get out more. This isn't 1995, Jilly. Kids are hooking up."

"*You* are hooking up." I make a face into the phone.

Lara's undergrads are interested in things like intersectionality and gender fluidity and personal agency, and I try to keep up. She's having a hard time balancing the two men she's sleeping with. Each of them wants her to be exclusive.

"My students say they can tell right away."

"Tell what?"

"When they're in a sex-positive place."

"A what?"

"A place that doesn't shame their bodies and what their bodies want to do. You could decide to be this."

"Be what?"

"You could be a sex-positive house."

"A sex-positive house. Thank you for this. Thanks for this lesson in sexual semiotics."

*Semiotics* was a word we liked to make fun of in art school, because what did it really mean? It was like a word that meant something no one really understood and that no one where I came from cared about.

I tell her I'm worried Sam is going quiet on me again.

She says, "It's Kit's accident. It's making Sam think about Liam again. What Sam needs right now is more radical empathy from you."

I do not know this term, *radical empathy,* and I tell Lara this.

She says radical empathy is the kind of empathy that makes you feel you completely understand someone else's life. "Like you're almost living their story."

She often gives me things to think about that I haven't thought of before, and these things live in my subconscious where I can't shake them. She has a cultish following of students who love her, and I love her too. But I tell her that I didn't realize she'd gotten a degree in psychotherapy.

She laughs.

"Lara, I've had so much empathy for Sam it's almost radical.

Please don't talk to me about more empathy. I have almost no control over my son anymore, in case you hadn't noticed."

"I'm very sorry, but you never had any control over either of your boys to begin with, and you need to finally understand this."

Then she says she has to hang up and pay the toll. She and the media-arts professor she's sleeping with are on their way to New York City to see a Laurie Anderson show. Lara is forever on road trips.

ONCE SHE AND I drove all day to get to her family's trailer up near the Canadian border, because her younger brother had enlisted in the army and was giving us his CD player. All he'd asked for in exchange was some rum.

This was at the end of the Dirty Dancing summer. Kit had taken me to his island in his boat the day before, and then Lara and I got in her Corolla the next morning and drove away. I wasn't sure I'd ever see him again.

She'd bought a small bongo drum at one of the county fairs, and I tapped the drum in my lap and sang to the radio and took photos out the window of the fields and farms and churches.

At one point she tried to explain her parents' evangelicalism to me, and said they believed girls should do only girls' work.

"What is girls' work?"

"Darning." She blew her cigarette smoke out the window. "Churning butter."

"You're lying." I let the Nikon hang from the strap around my neck. It was the camera my mother had bought for me. She always believed good things required money, and she told me she wasn't sure how, but the camera would help me leave the state one day.

"I wasn't allowed to listen to rock music or wear pants."

"For real?"

"For real."

I kept coming back to Kit in my mind, and to his tapered fingers and the rough skin on his face. It had been the greatest summer of my life.

Lara said she was so tired of the way her parents quietly oppressed her, while her brother got to do what he wanted. She knew they weren't going to give us the CD player without one of their religious screeds, and that we were going to need some of her brother's rum to get through it.

We stopped for gas at a convenience store in a field surrounded by gutted cars, and a teenage boy at the gas pump said Lara's Toyota was like a clown car because there were so many pretty girls getting out. But really there were just two of us, walking into the convenience store in our flip-flops like we owned it. We grabbed Twizzlers and Cokes.

When we got back in the car, the boy at the pump yelled, "You're all so damn pretty!"

I thought I was someone who became pretty by being around other pretty people like Lara. I got this feeling that I was distanced from my body, and I hoped that she and I could get over the whole pretty thing soon. Then she squealed the tires, and we blew kisses at the boy.

THAT NIGHT I MAKE meatballs with egg and ricotta cheese as a peace offering for Charlie. He loves these meatballs. I'm hoping that in exchange for the meatballs, he won't ask me to leave the house for Lucy and him.

Sam calls me on his friend Robbie's cell phone and says, "Guess what I got on my math test?"

"Sam." I grab a dish towel and wipe the raw hamburger meat off my hands.

"Guess again, Mom."

"Okay. A ninety-one."

"And again."

"Eighty."

"Way off."

I can hear Robbie in the background laughing. Robbie's father runs Maine Savings Bank, and Robbie seems to attend school half time and to play Fortnite the other half.

"Sam, I don't care what you got on your math test, but you're now making me care. How about you got a seventy?"

"Lower."

"Now I'm mad, Sam."

"Sixty-two."

"Say goodbye to Robbie and get in the boat and come home."

Robbie lives in one of the new McMansions on the mainland, with an electric gate and turrets. It's a ten-minute walk from our dock, and it takes Sam exactly eighteen minutes to get down to the rowboat and row across the channel.

"Don't do that again, please," I say when he walks in.

"Do what?"

"Don't go to Robbie's house when you should be writing your English essay, and don't call me about the math test you got an F on because you were smoking pot in the parking lot at McDonald's."

The meatballs are done, but they feel like a reward for Sam when there shouldn't be a reward.

"Wow. You're like completely out of control. What are you even saying? This is *exactly* why I called you and told you about my math test, to stop you from being mad to my face."

"Well, now I'm madder to your face than I would have been if you hadn't called. Why don't you study? Why don't you take yourself seriously? And what about your English essay?"

"I do take myself seriously, thank you very much. I take music seriously. I take basketball seriously. I finished the hubris essay after school with Mrs. Curtis."

It's like I haven't heard him, I'm so worked up.

"What's your hobby, Sam? Oh, wait. I forgot. It's Instagram."

Charlie comes out of my bedroom then. "Why are you being mean to him?"

"Because Sam called me from Robbie's and made me guess that he got a sixty-two on his math test."

I'm trying to adhere to the say-very-little strategy, but when Sam gets to me I can't help myself.

"Stupid move, Sam." Charlie fills his glass at the sink. "Really dumb. She'll always get mad at you for calling her like that. Always."

I put the meatballs on the table, and Sam picks one up in his fingers. It's as if he never learned to use a fork.

Kit and I have tried to teach him about cutlery. Even Neanderthals had forks.

"Sam." I hold up my fork. "This is a fork. Spelled *F-O-R-K*."

He smiles.

"Good one, Mom," Charlie says.

At least I've gotten them both to laugh.


AFTERWARD I MAKE THEM do the dishes.

When Sam stands up, he looks taller than he did yesterday.

He says, "I hate dishes."

"We all hate them, honey."

"Except Dad, who finds them *relaxing*." He takes the lid off the compost under the sink and starts scraping the plates and handing them to Charlie. "I hate the seagulls too. God, they like to shit on the boat."

"Don't say *shit*."

"*Shit* means excrement, Mom. It's okay to say *shit*."

"It's a swearword, and we don't swear." I hand him the dish towel.

"Did I say I hate doing the dishes?" Sam smiles at me.

I go outside in my slippers to look for whales in the dark. The trees are tall black shadows, and the wind whips the whitecaps into little peaks.

I walk back inside when I can't feel my toes. I say, "I never imagined in my wildest dreams that my children would swear so casually."

"Jillian." Sam talks in his serious voice now. "Swearing is only *normal*." He finishes drying the salad bowl and puts it on the counter upside down. "It's what teens *do*. They swear."

I ignore him.

Charlie says, "North Korea is about to launch another missile over the China Sea, Mom." He's still over at the sink. "Did you know this?"

"I do know this. The leader of North Korea is crazy. Please, please pour out all that water in the bathroom, Charlie. It looks like a bomb's gone off in there."

I GO INTO MY bedroom and change into sweatpants and call Kit from the bed.

He answers, which is sort of a miracle because he doesn't believe in cell phones. He has a smartphone, but Charlie says it isn't really smart because Kit does not let it do smart things.

"Pain report?" I ask him. "How bad today?"

The thing I worry most about is his pain, and how he doesn't ask for help when it gets to be too much.

He tells me he's very busy and can he call me back? Then he laughs. "All I do is physical therapy. Lift the weights up. Put the weights down. Push the weights in. Pull the weights out. When are you coming?"

"Friday. We'll be there Friday."

He's in a better mood today, but I've decided not to tell him about the joint and the car and McDonald's. I don't need to protect my husband. It's just easier while he's in the hospital.

But then I can't stop myself. It's impossible for me to keep a secret from him.

I say, "You need to brace yourself, but Sam was smoking pot at McDonald's last week while I was up there with you, and he put it on Instagram."

"What do you mean, 'put it on Instagram'?"

"The photo. He posted it."

"Nice, Sam. Let me talk to him. Why don't you put *him* on?" Kit coughs. "Let me explain some things about pot and the law and stupidity."

I get up and stand in the doorway and wave Sam over.

He's in his LeBron James jersey, making something at the counter involving peanut butter and cheese and pretends he doesn't see me.

I put my hand over the phone and hiss, "Please get over here."

He slides to the doorway in his socks and takes the phone.

"Hey, Dad," he says, and smiles the smile I haven't seen in days.

Then he lies on my bed with the phone for what seems like an hour, while I sit on the couch and look at old seed catalogues and think about the night Sam got stopped for speeding back in August.

At the time it hadn't seemed like a big thing. His new friend Roman was with him in the car, and Sam had only had his license a month, so it was illegal for Roman to be in the car. The cop who pulled them over made them both get out and stand on the side of the road in the dark behind the Sedgewick cliffs.

Then the cop had climbed into the Subaru to search for drugs, but all he found was a pack of clove cigarettes. He asked Sam how old he was, and Sam said sixteen.

The cop said sixteen was too young to smoke cloves or Mary Jane or anything else, so from now on he'd call Sam "Shit for Brains."

"Okay?" the cop had said. "Okay, Shit for Brains?"

Sam hadn't known whether to agree or not.

He had explained all this to me while I sat in my wooden chair behind the house in the dark, searching for whales. He told me that he'd said nothing to the cop. Then the cop said, "I didn't hear you. When I say Shit for Brains, you say okay. Okay, Shit for Brains?"

"You smoke *cloves?*" I'd interrupted him. "Cloves? Sam. How gross."

"Mom," he'd said, as if this was an answer to my question.

I had to take it as a yes, which is one of the concessions I'm still learning about with the teenagers, where you receive the bad information like the cloves and wait for what's really coming, which is inevitably worse.

The cop had made Roman and Sam stand side by side on the road near the estuary and promise they'd never smoke anything ever again.

"No *Mary Jane,*" Sam had said to me in his ironic voice, and smiled. Then he got up from the grass where he'd been sitting next to me and went inside.

Overall, I felt the conversation had gone pretty well, and I was truly relieved. I wasn't as wrung out or fried as I usually was after talking with Sam about hard things, and I believed he'd told me the truth.

I'd called Kit that night. The boat was back in port, so he answered from the room in the basement where he slept at Dyer's house. I said I didn't want to worry him, but a strange cop down from Augusta who no one seemed to know in Sewall had just pulled Sam over, and it sounded like police harassment. "I mean, he called Sam Shit for Brains."

"He did what?" Kit had laughed and laughed and seemed almost happy Sam had been pulled over. "It's good if he got scared a little, Jilly. Don't baby him."

"But Shit for Brains? There's something creepy about it."

"The cop was just trying to scare a boy. I'll talk to Sam. I'll set him straight. Put him on. Get him on the phone."

"He's up in bed. Wiped."

Then I told Kit that I loved him and missed him so much I could not say.

When I'd woken up in the dark later, I could hear the lapping sound of the water on the rocks. I love that sound. It's the sound I want to die listening to. But I was certain then that Sam had been smoking pot in the car, and that he and Roman had just hidden it from the cop well. Or maybe the cop had found the pot, and this was why he'd called Sam Shit for Brains. Either way, I saw how Sam had probably lied to me, which was the really scary thing.

I'VE GONE THROUGH ALL the old seed catalogues by the time Sam comes out of my bedroom.

"It was a good talk?"

"All good." He nods.

It takes restraint not to press for more. The LeBron jersey is so big on him it's like a dress, and I have to work hard not to smile at his skinny legs.

He asks if I want to do A-Reader, which is short for the Archer Family Reading Hour he named three years ago. It's a way to say he'd like to read with me without having to say he'd like to read with me. A sweet leftover from when he was young that he hasn't let go of.

I follow him back to my bedroom and take the left side of the bed, near the door. Sam takes Kit's side, near the window. Talking is against the rules during A-Reader. You just read.

I've started a book about Robert Scott's doomed trip to the South Pole, written by a crew member who found Scott's dead body.

Sam's reading *The Hunger Games* again. I think it's his third time and that he finds the story soothing. Though what this says about his anxiety, I almost don't want to know. We made him wait until he was twelve before we gave it to him. Kit read it first to see if it was okay. He reported that he saw no way we could keep it from Sam. It's hard to keep anything from Sam. He's always in our business. The best part was how he lit up when we finally said yes.

Every few minutes now he laughs at something in the book and takes some barbecue potato chips from the bag he's brought into bed.

Charlie comes in and lies down on top of us, and we can't really move our arms. We stay like this for several minutes, sort of suffocating. Then Charlie starts reading the book with Sam, turning the pages for him.

In profile Charlie looks even more like his father: same square jaw and eyebrows so thick and dark you think they're pretend.

"How would you choose to die?" Sam asks him. "Early in the war? Or would you walk into the woods and die later?"

"Sam," I say. "Please."

I'm feeling jumpy about Robert Scott's chances at the South Pole. His crew is exhausted. "Do we really have to talk about death?"

"The woods," Charlie says, ignoring me. "I'd walk into the woods."

Then he buries his head in my shoulder. I can't tell if this is an expression of spontaneous emotion or if his nose itches. I don't care. I don't move.

Charlie smells like toast and something sugary that must be his new hair gel.

"Me too," Sam says. "I'd choose to die in the woods."

Charlie thinks it's too crowded in the bed, and he climbs out and stands at the window and looks at the ocean.

"It's like you and Dad are divorced or something," he says. "Dad's been gone so long."

"It's not like that at all." But my heartbeat ticks up, because of how big Kit's absence feels.

I close my book and tell the boys they can leave Maine when

they grow up, but they can never go to the South Pole. "It's too dangerous. I forbid it."

They both assure me that they won't travel to the South Pole. Sam goes so far as to say that he is *reluctantly* taking the South Pole off his bucket list. I know he doesn't have a bucket list.

I stare out the window and see Kit far at sea with no one to save him. He is someone who would go to the South Pole. He's never been afraid of the ocean.

When this gets too scary to think about, I climb out of bed. Some of the potato chips spill on the sheet.

Charlie slides back into the bed and laughs at how easy it is to trick me into giving up my spot.

LATER I FOLLOW SAM up to the loft, where the ceiling slants down so low over his bed that it's like I'm talking to the poster of Kevin Durant from the Brooklyn Nets.

"What's the deal, Sam? What's with the pot?"

"It was a one-time thing. It was an *experiment.*"

"Tell me the experiment's over." I stare at Kevin Durant's kind-looking eyes.

"It's over."

"Promise me. Because I can't take it right now, Sam. I can't. It's not happening. Are we clear?"

"Clear."

"No friends after school and no phone for the week."

"You're hard-core, Jillian."

"Don't call me Jillian. Call me Mom. I'm your mom. Your mother."

"Well, I was about to tell you we need a microphone, *Mom,* and an equalizer for the band. It'll cost like five hundred dollars, and could you loan me? Could you do that, please? Please please? We'll be practicing at Roman's house like every day once I'm *ungrounded.*"

I try not to laugh.

"What you need is to not smoke pot ever again in the McDonald's parking lot, because if you do, you won't have a phone or a life, much less an equalizer or new microphone."

It's important to be almost solemn with him.

Then I cry a little.

"Don't cry, Mom."

This is when I see that I have him. "Who's Roman?"

"New. Croatia. Tall. Basketball. Did you know that I'm almost ready to leave this place?"

"Leave when?" I look around the room. There's just enough space to cram in the old bureau I painted and his single bed. "We're on an island, in case I need to remind you."

"You should be ready." He pulls the covers up to his chin. "You should watch out. Any day now. Robbie and Roman and me. Burlington, Vermont. I need to get away from this family and go do radical things."

I want to tell him I'm not holding my breath.

"What I want is for you to get a good night's sleep."

"I have worries."

"Tell me." I close my eyes. "Tell me about your worries. Tell me." It feels like every muscle in my body is flexed now.

"I can't."

"No, you can." I look at him. "You absolutely can. You can tell me anything."

"I just need sleep. I just need to talk to Dad again."

He rolls over, and several minutes go by during which I rub his back and feel how close I got to his secrets and then how far away again.

"If I come back as another person after I die," he says, "will I still have my same personality?"

"I think you will."

"I want to. I want to still be me." He's been saying this last part for years.

I rub his back some more.

Then he asks me to do his feet and his Achilles tendons, which ache from all the running at basketball practice. He says he promises not to smoke pot and to always be on time for his classes.

I'm flooded with love for him.

I leave him and poke my head in Charlie's room.

He says *Tom Sawyer* is better than *Gulliver's Travels,* last semester's English book. "*Tom Sawyer*'s good, even." The book is propped up on his knees. "But the writing can be dense and hard to understand."

"Harder than Shakespeare?"

"Tom gets in real trouble. He gets punished."

"I don't think my children know what punishment is."

"Goodnight, Mom. Goodbye," he says, maybe by way of not having an argument with me over what punishment is.

He looks like an old man under the quilt. I make a pact with myself to try to pay more attention to him, because Sam takes up so much room.

I go to hug him, but he waves me off. He's been doing this more since he started dating Lucy.

It's true that Kit and I rarely really punish the boys. I know Jimmy thinks it's a fault of ours. But even Jimmy's grown softer because of the boys.

"By the way, Mom," Charlie says, "Robbie smokes pot."

I can't really hear him. "He what?"

"Robbie dabs."

"And so?" It's late. I don't really know what the word *dab* means, but I can't appear uninformed.

"It's only a matter of time," he says.

"Until what?"

"Until Sam is doing it too."

"There you go again. Parenting him. I hate when you do this."

"The good news is they're all still scared of you."

"Who are?"

"Robbie and Roman and Derrick."

"Scared of me?"

"We all are." He laughs then.

"Good." I smile at him.

## PART THREE

## *BELIEVE*

AFTER KIT AND I moved to the island, I got a grant from the state to teach filmmaking at the youth prison. There weren't many girls in this prison. Only three or four, because they don't like to put girls in prison. But there were lots of boys. Almost one hundred of them, broken up into pods down these locked cinder-block wings.

I took *The Duchess* to the mainland two days a week and drove to the prison with old video cameras. The boys made short animation films and did documentary-style interviews. They were starving for things to do and desperate to get out. They wanted people—adults, their parents, anyone at all—to save them.

"Please save me," a boy named Michael always said to me when he got up to go to the bathroom during class.

Some of the boys had done bad things, and some had done very bad things, and none of them were beyond repair. I really felt this way and wanted to tell the guards and the prison director with the orange beard that if only the boys could get a little more.

A little more what? Kit asked me one night when I came home from the prison and sat in the wooden chair outside looking for whales.

More attention, maybe, I said. Or respect? Though what I'd say now if he asked is that the boys just needed to be seen. It's not complicated. Needing to be seen.

There was one guard who never smiled and never let the boys talk in line on their way back to their pods, and I wanted to tell him that the boys weren't who he thought they were, and that it was wrong to think boys lacked feeling or remorse. Because really they were quiet and scared.

Some had mental illnesses, and some had very bad parents, and all of them needed treatment, and wasn't that easy to see? It was easy.

It was more complicated than that though, and I knew it. But I wanted to keep my feelings about the boys in prison simple.

Once when I was leaving the prison there was a fire alarm and the prison went on lockdown so no one could get in or out. This sounds counterintuitive. If there was a fire in a prison, you'd want to unlock the doors and let the children out, but the alarm had been pulled so many times for things that weren't fires that the guards no longer believed the alarm.

When the alarm went off, I was upstairs in the area where parents waited for visiting hours. I hated being locked in. Hated it, but I could see the blue sky outside and the Subaru in the parking lot, and I knew I'd drive away soon.

A man and a woman waited in there with me. They were white and thirty-something and strung out on opiates maybe. Slurring and with unkempt hair. I could hear them talking at the check-in desk to the guard with the gun at his hip. Their son had been released the day before but not to them, and he hadn't come home, and they'd been expecting him.

This was the year before Charlie was born, 2001. I couldn't understand how the parents didn't know where their boy was. Their little boy. In a way they were all little boys in there. Even the ones who'd done the most horrible things had also experienced horrible things done to them.

·   ·   ·

THEN CHARLIE WAS BORN, and Sam very soon after Charlie. I didn't work at the prison anymore. It seemed like a foreshadowing of how badly things could go.

Sometimes I felt guilty that Charlie and Sam collected mussel shells while the boys in the prison were desperate for someone to save them, but Kit and I couldn't afford day care.

I was often alone with the boys when they were babies. It took several years to figure out the balance between taking care of them and making the films. What I really mean is that I never figured out the balance. The boys always caught me by surprise with what they required. The amounts of love and attention, and I still think of those years sometimes as the lost years. Or the years I was invisible.

ONCE WHEN HE WAS seven, Sam cornered me in the kitchen and told me I'd waited too long to have him.

"Twenty-nine years old," he said with his serious face. "Way, way too late."

"What are you even talking about?" It was July and so hot I'd made cold tomato soup and given them cold cereal and anything else cold I thought they'd eat.

We'd covered the island two times inspecting raccoon droppings and bear droppings, even though there were no bears, but it was still exciting to talk about them.

I was okay being alone on the island with the boys, because I knew Kit was coming back. I could count the days and dole myself out to the boys in this way. This was after the rougher time, when the boys were both babies, and I thought I was going crazy out there alone and had nothing to dole out because I was so tired.

"Dumb dumb dumb," Sam said.

He wore the towel cape and muck boots and Charlie's cutoffs, and he had made holsters out of rope and felt. The metal pipes in the holsters were stuck together with wads of masking tape. "When I'm fifty, you'll be almost eighty, and then you'll die, and we won't have a relationship anymore."

I stared at him. "Is this what you think of? Our relationship?"

I had the mess of tomatoes to clean up, but I should have taken him more seriously. This is what I often think about Sam. If I just take him more seriously, I can solve him. But then I run out of time or get distracted, and the puzzle of him starts over again.

"It was *stupid,* Mom. You didn't plan well."

"What was stupid?" I can be slow like this.

"To have me so late. You won't know me or my kids."

Oh God. Who was he? What was this malarkey? He was seven.

"But I know you *now.* Besides. I'm going to live till I'm a hundred."

He seemed disgusted with this statement, as if he knew it was my Hail Mary. Then he turned on his heels and left.

SOMETIMES THERE ARE NO Instagram posts. Then a series of videos by an ex-NBA player with mottled green tattoos who sells an enzyme drink called BELIEVE for rapid muscle growth.

ON WEDNESDAY MORNING WE'RE about five miles from school when I see the gas needle buried in empty. "I need to announce that I'm not sure we're going to make it to school today. LOL."

"Please don't ever talk in text like that again, Mom," Sam says from the backseat, where he's watching the trees. "Please."

I've started keeping a running list in my mind of things I need to do for the wolves. On bad days I call this the List of Resentments. I try not to think about the list. But my brain would have worked differently without the boys. I think it would have stayed more open, and that I would be making more films and not a List of Resentments.

I look at the trees through the dirty windshield. Really look at them. If I hadn't had the boys, my brain would have stayed freer.

It has to be chemical, because the boys have taken over my brain, but I would have them all over again if I could.

The big thing I want to report to Kit but can never find the right words to say on the phone is that the boys and I are not the same person. We never were. Sometimes it's like we're meeting one another for the first time, and they are not my friends or even my allies.

Hello, I imagine saying to them. Hello, I am your mother.

. . .

WE MAKE IT PAST the credit union. Charlie has a biology test he studied for until midnight. He wonders out loud why I didn't get gas earlier. Then he says he's not sure that he can take either of us anymore. Me or Sam. And that maybe he should move to Lucy's. "They all want me to."

"Oh really?" I am focused on the gas gauge. If we run out of gas, my credibility will be forever hurt.

"During the school year it would be much easier to live there than go back and forth to the island. All of Lucy's family want me to do it."

He's moving in with them and I haven't met Lucy yet?

I tell him he's unfair and that he was the last one to drive the Subaru, and that if he says one more word about the gas, I'll pull over and he'll have to get out and walk.

No one speaks after this.


WE ROLL INTO DALE'S Service Station, and my hands are shaking when I unscrew the gas cap. It's the fastest I've gotten gas.

Charlie is only three minutes late to school.

He jumps out before I park.

Then I get out too, because it's the day of Sam's parent-teacher conference.

He tells me on the sidewalk it will be better if I don't talk during it. Then he smiles.

"Like not say anything? I have to say something."

The high school is made of dark red brick and smells of unidentified lunch meat. It's where Kit and Jimmy went to school, but this history doesn't seem to be anything Sam takes pride in.

We climb the cement stairs and wedge ourselves into the brown laminated desks with attached metal chairs, and Mrs. Curtis smiles at us and thanks us for being there. She's sixtyish, with short, feathered hair like a grown-up Dorothy Hamill.

Then she holds up a black attendance book in her hand and tells me that Sam has ten tardies and eight absences since school started this year.

She pauses to let that sink in. "It is only October thirtieth."

I don't understand at first what I'm looking at.

Mrs. Curtis uses a yellow pencil to walk me through the columns. There are so many days that I thought Sam was in school when he wasn't at school I can't understand.

I don't look at Sam. I just look at the columns. But I can't control what my face is doing.

"Not bad, Sam. Pretty impressive, really." But my heart's in my throat, because where has he been when he hasn't been in school?

"We are reading Shakespeare," Mrs. Curtis says. "Sam has important things to say that he is not saying, because he is rarely in class."

I nod. How did I let him wear that torn Clash T-shirt, and why hasn't he cut his hair?

"When Sam *does* talk, he often makes good comments, but then he disparages his comments, which sets a tone for the class and sabotages any good points he made earlier."

"But the girls already know everything," he says. "They know all the answers, so it's not even worth it to talk."

I look at Mrs. Curtis and want to remind her about the bridge and Liam and to tell her that Sam has come pretty far and that he's better than this. Better than Mrs. Curtis thinks.

But there is no chance to talk, really, because Mrs. Curtis speaks quickly.

"You're a leader of the class, Sam. You can figure out how to handle five girls. The others follow your cue."

Here she turns and speaks directly to me. "He talks over me

and under me, Mrs. Archer. I can't seem to get him to quiet down." Then she stares at Sam for a moment through her reading glasses, which are attached to a long brass chain that hangs around her neck. "I really thought he'd be my leader." She shakes her head.

I find this the saddest part, because Mrs. Curtis uses the past tense. As if we've already lost Sam to the band in Burlington, Vermont.

I want to tell him that each time he skips school, he lies to me.

Mrs. Curtis says that she'd like to see a better system in our family for getting Sam to school. She's relying on Kit and me to make this work.

"We've got some things going on at home," I try to tell her.

She stands and nods the kind of nod that implies the Archers always have things going on at home. Then she thanks us for coming in.

When we're out in the hall of lockers, Sam says, "What's truancy, Mom?"

I can't breathe very well. I want to yell things at him and go on a little rant. But whenever I try yelling at him he looks amused, which masks the genuine hurt I think he feels that anyone would ever dare yell at him in the first place. So then I'm up against willful ignorance and righteous indignation.

I don't answer except to say he's walking home after school. I'm not coming to get him.

"That's impossible, Mom. We live on an island, remember?"

"Well, you will have to figure that out, then."

I HAVE AN APPOINTMENT with Katherine at Hair Creations in the little strip mall across town. On the way over there I call Nettie, the school social worker, and leave a message telling her that we have another problem with Sam. Nettie hasn't seen Sam in over a year, but I know she'll understand.

Then I sit in Katherine's black vinyl chair, and she tells me that she can't take the Maine winters any longer and is moving to Orlando.

I ask if I can go with her.

I'm so angry at Sam. So angry. Then my worry outweighs my anger. Then my love outweighs my worry. It goes in a circle. Anger. Worry. Love.

I don't know if you can flunk out of high school for not going. Maybe you just get held back a year.

I ask Katherine to cut my hair shorter but piecey on the sides. "Please don't do anything that makes me look middle-aged."

She shakes her blond mane over her shoulders. "I'll do a bob that angles up in the back."

"I'm afraid of bobs. Aren't bobs middle-aged?" I can see in the mirror what a bad shade of charcoal my hair is, and how it poofs out around my face. I should never have dyed it.

"Okay. What I'm going to do to your hair will never be confused with a bob."

But then she gives me a bob. Now I look middle-aged. It's as if she's already left for Florida and didn't hear anything I said. My hair is short and frizzy, and soon I'll be wearing mom jeans and Lara will evacuate me.


I DRIVE BACK DOWN to the village, and the whole time my head is worry worry worry. I pull into the dirt landing next to the store and call Kit on my cell.

He doesn't answer.

Why have a phone, really?

There's a stillness in the village this morning. Everyone is out on their boats or down at the pier or has gotten jobs in town if they had to.

I call Candy, and she comes out the side door of the store in her red robe with the New England Patriots coffee mug in her left hand. It's hard to believe she's already fed a couple dozen lobstermen in the dark. Or that after the first round she went upstairs and napped and is now starting over again.

She's short and wiry like Jimmy, with a soft, round face like her mother's, and long copper-colored hair.

"What on earth?" she says.

"Just look at me, will you!" I push the car door open.

She puts the mug on the car roof and presses my hair down with both her hands, then shakes her head.

"I look like Charlie, don't I? I bet I look like Charlie."

"Charlie's handsome, so I don't know what you're complaining about. But you're right." She leans on the car door. "It is not a good haircut."

I push my driving glasses up on my head and try to tell her about Sam and the joint in the Instagram post and the school conference.

"Why is he so defiant? I mean, this was never me. Who is he?"

"He's all Jimmy." Candy crosses her arms above her chest.

"Sam is *all* Jimmy." Then she pats my back. "Jesus, Mary, Joseph. Someone cut this family a break."

She reaches for my hand and tries to pull me up. "Come in. Come have a coffee while I get dressed. Come."

I shake my head. "I shouldn't even be here. I should be up at the hospital."

"You need rest. I'll go. Flip and I will go."

"I'm taking the boys up on Friday."

Flip comes out then and waves and gets in his pickup. He's tall and completely bald and is less volatile than Jimmy but no less impassioned about keeping the village a working village. I finally filmed him last month and got him to tell me his father's stories about the hundreds of thousands of cod that used to come up through Sewall in great migrations.

Flip said the boats came from as far away as Russia with giant nets, and that when we finally put a stop to it, it was probably too late.

Candy bends down and hugs me. She's a hugger, like Kit. It's surprising the way they hug, and I attribute it to their mother. But Candy also withholds important information like Kit does. Even after her second glass of chardonnay, she's never told me what really happened the day their mother died. I know it's a Maine thing, this withholding. But sometimes it seems like a competition to see how much bad news you can take without cracking.

I STEER *The Duchess* back to the island. The sun still isn't fully down yet, and the sky is a soft gray. Everything looks peaceful on the water, and I have some time to think about who I want to be when I get to the house.

Sam and Charlie are both lying on the rug in front of the

woodstove. Don't ask me how either of them got home. Sam is actually reading his Shakespeare.

I ask him to fry bacon for the pasta. This is the one thing I say to him. If I say anything else, I'll say too much. At least I know this about myself.

He gets up and turns the burner on and stares at me. "You don't look like you, Mom. I think your hair's too short."

I can't believe that he dares talk to me.

Then he says, "Please hurry dinner. I'm so hungry. Hungrier than ever before in my life. The most starving ever."

"Good, because I'm making mushroom soup." I stir the pasta. "And pasta with mushroom sauce."

"Really, Mom?" He squeezes his hands together by the stove. "You know I can't stand mushrooms!"

I think he's going to cry.

Charlie can't keep the joke going any longer and laughs, and that breaks it.

Then Sam picks me up from behind. "Good one, Mom. Good one. You really got me!"

"Put me down and set the table." I try not to smile.

He takes the blue plates down from the shelf. "But really, what did you do to your hair, Mom?"

"It will grow." I bring the pasta over to the table.

The boys sit down. They're not listening to me anymore. They're eating like they've never seen pasta before and have stopped caring about my hair, if they ever cared.

"I need to grow," Sam says, almost to himself, and takes another big bite of pasta. "I really, really need to grow. Like today."

WHEN IT'S SO DARK out that I can't tell the sky from the ocean, I lie on my bed and make Sam confess where he was when he wasn't at school.

He says he was at Roman's.

"But I don't even know Roman."

"I told you. He's a senior. His dad's maybe an electrician. I think his mom works at a hair salon."

"It's nice you have a new friend, but you've got to go to school. You know that, right?"

"You really don't have to worry about me. Please stop."

"I just want you trying at school." I take his hand. "School is everything. Dad wants you in school. I want you at school. Why don't you see that?"

He stands up, and his sweatpants come down to his calves. "But my brain doesn't *like* school. You know that! I'm stupid at school."

"Don't talk like that, Sam Archer."

I want to warn him that some people, maybe not Mrs. Curtis but other people, will have low expectations for him because he's a boy. I've seen the way people sell boys out, and he should trust me on this.

"You will check in with Mrs. Curtis in homeroom every day. And you will check in with Nettie. We will all know if you're not there."

He asks me again when Dad is coming home.

I tell him that it's up to the doctors.

He shakes his head. "Who are these doctors, anyway?"

"You'll see them on Friday. You can ask them yourself."

He shakes his head again and goes into the kitchen and fries some salami and two eggs.

Charlie's on the couch now reading The Princeton Review's *Complete Book of Colleges.* He says the salami looks like a plate of grease.

"Actually, no," he says. "It's a grease bomb."

"It's delicious." Sam takes a bite. "So please shut up."

Then Charlie makes something he calls tuna supreme, which involves a can of tuna and sliced pickles with a glob of mayo on top. He's wearing the gray Champion sweatpants and a blue sweatshirt with the hood up, so he looks like a boxer, even though Charlie hates boxing. Last month he announced a weight-gain plan involving eating as many calories after dark as he can.

Sam says, "Your tuna supreme looks grosser than my fried salami, dude."

"Good people," Charlie announces, "all I am trying to do is find something to eat in this house."

VERY EARLY ON THURSDAY morning I tell Charlie how Sam's been skipping school. I've got to tell someone. It's thirty-three degrees out. I have on two sweaters and the amoeba coat. The ocean looks like a bluish-gray animal that keeps changing shapes.

"Sam's in tenth grade." Charlie stokes the woodstove. "You don't fool around in tenth grade. You *listen*." He goes back to the table, where he's preparing for a gun-control debate.

"Mrs. Curtis told me that Sam is a leader, and when he says negative things, the other kids in class say negative things too. Then the class is lost."

I shouldn't confide in my seventeen-year-old, but it feels good.

"Sam isn't a leader," Charlie says. "I've never seen a moment when he's been a leader."

Sam comes down in old blue sweatpants with no shirt on and stomps into the bathroom and turns on the handheld shower. The pipes make the screeching sound again.

"Please go with me on this, Charlie." I pour the boiling water into the French press. "You need to understand that Sam is a leader when you're not around."

"When has he *ever* led? Give me one example." He laughs, and I can see all his teeth—the straight ones on top and the bottom ones that are trying to crowd each other out.

"It's just not your style of leading. It's different. It's not like when you lead."

. . .

ONCE WHEN CHARLIE WAS six he found me in the garden behind the house and told me that he'd taught Sam how to swim.

"How did you do that?" I asked, and stared at his dripping shorts.

I'd been trying to get Sam to swim for months.

"It was easy. I pushed him off the rocks. Then he swam back to shore."

"Wow." I went back to the gardening. I didn't want to hear about anything else Charlie had done that would later implicate me.

"Yeah. Wow." He wouldn't meet my eyes. He looked guilty but like he'd discovered some power he hadn't known he had.

AFTER I TAKE THE boys to school, I stop at Shaw's and get the food Charlie will cook with Lucy.

"And this bothers you why?" Lara asks when I call her on my way back to the island and tell her that I'm leaving Charlie and Lucy alone in the house tonight and taking Sam to Candy's for dinner. "Your son is seventeen."

"My mother would die if she knew I was doing this."

Lara strikes a match. "You have to decide."

"Decide what?"

"If you're going to be a sex-positive house."

"I thought I already was sex-positive."

"Oh, you are sex-positive, but now it's whether your house is going to be. Or if you're going to pass the shame or blame about sex onto this girl Lucy. The same shame that's been passed on to girls forever."

"Oh please."

"No, really. It's whether you're going to make Lucy and Charlie feel bad about their bodies."

"Jesus, Lara."

"Yeah, I know."

"Okay, okay."

I park under the trees and carry the bags of food down to *The Duchess* and putt across the channel. The sky is a pinkish gray. I tie the boat at the float and lug the bags up to the house and put most of the food away. Then I start editing the film. I have almost five hours of footage to get through today.

Charlie and Sam row home in the afternoon, and Charlie opens the fridge and does a survey of yogurt and pickles and milk.

"Thank you for shopping, Mom," he says. "But I don't think there's anything here for Lucy and me to actually *eat*."

"Look, Charlie." Sam holds up a bag of spelt bread. "You can have pickles and honey on a piece of spelt."

"But you know how much I hate spelt, Mom," Charlie says.

Are those tears in his eyes?

"Stop. There's good food here. I worked hard to get this food for you guys. Please stop. There's steak in the fridge. There are potatoes."

"Phew," Charlie says, and lies down on the couch.

Sam goes up to his room to do who knows what.

I yell up the ladder that he should pack before we go to Candy's, because we're leaving for Canada early the next morning.


BUT THEN THE SKY darkens, and the wind picks up, and the boats slam against the float. No one is able to go anywhere. The water's too rough.

Charlie still begs me to let him go get Lucy.

"Are you looking at the same whitecaps I'm looking at?" I ask him. "Do you see that wind?"

He lies on the couch with his eyes closed.

"I'm sorry. I know you're disappointed. I know how much this meant to you."

He doesn't open his eyes, but he says, "It's really hard to get her here. Her mom almost didn't let her come. You don't even know Lucy's mom yet. You should know her. She's amazing. She's raising Lucy's brothers and sister on her own. You should meet her."

"That would be nice. I'd love to meet Lucy's mother."

I go into my bedroom and stand at the window and look at the storm. Then I call Kit. It's a wonder that Charlie taught him how to answer his phone. God forbid he should try to FaceTime or Skype. There's never any way to see him.

"What have I ever done to the boys," I tell him when he answers, "except feed them and buy them cell phones? Sometimes Sam doesn't speak to me all day."

"Most teenage boys don't speak. We've made it this far without trouble, Jilly."

"I don't consider this very far. Sam isn't even sorry. I mean, he put the picture on Instagram. Who does that?"

"But you smoked pot, Jilly."

"Pot hated me. I always thought I was dying. I should have had girls."

I go into the kitchen and try to talk to Kit and pull a garbage bag out of the can under the sink at the same time. Then I hear a dog bark.

"Who's that?"

"Maxwell's barking at some squirrel out the window."

"Maxwell?"

I hear Marsh tell the dog to get off Kit's bed. I can't recover after that. I've pictured him alone up there. Solitary. Just waiting to come home. There's a silence on the line while I wish Marsh away. She brings out a jealousy I didn't know I had.

The sky is drained of color and looks like a black cloth that no light will ever penetrate, and these gusts of wind blow through and almost lift the house up.

"The weather's bad," I finally say. "I need cash to buy Sam new basketball sneakers."

"Use the credit card, babe."

"The credit card is maxed out."

I wait. Then I say, "I can't believe you're in the hospital and we're arguing."

"We aren't arguing. Put Charlie on. Please put him on for me. I want to hear him."

"He's feeding the lizards."

When Charlie brings a lizard out of the terrarium like this, I worry it will run away and get lost in the house. He loves the lizards and knows everything about their digestive tracts and hydration needs and has names for each of them. Sometimes he complains that the lizards are taking over his life. But we can't ever lose them.

Sam and I call the lizards the Boys.

Kit helps with the Boys. They're his territory.

"Well, tell him to call me. Ask both boys why they don't call me."

"You're forgetting about their unformed frontal lobes, " I say. "They don't think about calling anyone." Charlie's lying on his back on the rug with the lizard in his left hand, and he smiles at me and nods.

"You could make them call."

"I'm having a hard enough time managing their sex lives and drug use."

He laughs, and Marsh's dog barks again.

Then he asks me what time we'll get there tomorrow.

"Three o'clock. I'm aiming for three. But it sounds like you already have plenty of company."

I hang up then.

After I do this I don't really know why I've done it.

"Well, someone seems upset," Charlie says.

"Your father and I were just having a conversation. That's what adults do, Charlie, they talk about things."

But my head feels underwater. I've read how jealousy reveals everything bad about the person who feels jealous.

"No, really," he says. "Why the mood?"

"I'm worried about your father."

Sometimes I think Charlie holds me to a higher standard and then I fail to meet this standard. He has no idea, really, what I've done or not done, but I think he can still somehow feel it when I've failed.

"Dad is *fine*." It's like he's talking to the lizard now, not to me. "Dad's a big boy. He'll be all right."

HERE IS A MEMORY: Kit takes me to a smaller island near his island with a white sand beach. These are the days before the boys are born. We're camping in the dunes above the beach, and we swim and pretend to read on the striped blanket, but I can't pay attention to the words because Kit's lying beside me in the sand with his hand on my hip. I have nothing to want because I have him and want him entirely.

BEFORE WE LEAVE FOR Canada, the boys and I go out to the trawler to batten things down. The nets and ropes and old, coffee-stained maps. A pilled fleece vest.

The boat is a haunted house to me. Cavernous. Forty feet of metal, with a mast that rises in the middle. It's a whole world, this boat. The deck is made of a coarse gray metal that we have to repaint every year. The controls are in the pilot house in the midship, with the steering wheel and gear throttle and electronics.

Sam loves anything to do with the trawler. Sometimes I think he believes it's his boat. He's the one who begs to go on fishing trips with Kit. He knows his way around the boat better than Charlie or I.

He bosses Charlie around now until the deck is pretty much cleared.

I'm down in the cabin, where it smells like bilge oil. There's an empty carton of Marlboros and a black transistor radio, and I feel like Kit is gone, gone now. Like he's dead or something. It's the oddest, worst feeling.

"Creepy," Charlie says from up on deck.

How did he know what I was thinking?

"Creepy how?" I say.

"Creepy how this bilge oil spread and we stepped in it," Sam says. He's standing next to his brother in his blue hoodie.

Then he jumps down into the cabin and gets very close to my face. "Who do you love more, Mom? Me or Charlie?"

I'm so surprised by this question. And sad. I hate it when Sam asks me this. "Both of you."

The boat rolls up and down on the swells, and I reach out my arm to balance against the hull.

"But can you even stand me?" Sam says.

"Sam, what are you saying?" I wipe my tears with my parka sleeve.

"Mom." Charlie climbs down with us. "Mom. Please don't cry, Mom." Then he looks at Sam. "Of course she loves me more."


LEBRON JAMES GOES MISSING back at the house, and Sam won't leave for Canada without him.

"Where is LeBron?" He stomps around the loft. "I can't find him!"

I finally find him at the bottom of the clothes basket in the bathroom. Sam puts him on and seems much better.

It's eight in the morning now. We get out of *The Duchess* and climb in the car and drive out to the highway. Charlie's in the front seat, texting or Snapchatting or whatever you call it. He keeps smiling and nodding at the screen, so it looks like an actual conversation, but not the kind I'm used to.

I've given Sam back his phone for the trip. He's in the back, listening to his music on it with earphones, blissed out. He says he's sure that Dad's coming home with us on Sunday. Nothing can sway him from this belief. But I've tracked down doctors and hospital people for hours this week, until it's felt like entire days, trying to understand the criteria for when Kit will be released, and I'm almost certain it won't be this Sunday.

Sam and Kit share a language. They like to get inside the minds of fish and talk about what the fish would do and where the fish would go. They say they have to think like fish. Then they place their gear in the water and wait.

Both boys need Kit. But Sam needs extra Kit before he becomes himself again and puts down the little axes he likes to grind.

AFTER BANGOR THE FIELDS stretch for miles, and there are stone walls and herds of cows and sheep. It feels like I'm driving to the end of the earth. It's good in this part of Maine, and so quiet it's like a dream.

When the boys wake up hours later, they stare blankly at the trees. We pass a gray barn on a hill. I've always wanted to live in a barn. So did my mother.

"Where are the cigarettes?" she used to say when I was in high school.

I'd go find her menthols in the junk drawer under the sink and wave them in the air.

"Let's head out to the patio," she'd say and laugh, because we did not have a patio.

We'd walk outside and smoke in the tent thingy with the mosquito netting that my father bought used from someone at the mill. She had the calmest voice and knew more about my longings than she let on.

When I told her yesterday that I was driving the boys up to see Kit, she said, "Well, of course you are."

"I THINK I'LL NEED to drink soon," Charlie says after Sam falls back asleep.

"Drink what?"

If the car breaks down now, I don't think that we'll be found in these woods for days.

"Alcohol. I need to see if I like it."

He's wearing an old sweatshirt of Kit's with the name of Jimmy's lobster pound on it. ARCHER'S is spelled in green block print across the chest. Candy had the sweatshirts made for everyone at the pound ten years ago.

Jimmy thought they were ridiculous. Who needed sweatshirts? Next thing you know, he said, we'll have bumper stickers. I'm not sure there's anything Jimmy hates more than bumper stickers.

"That's the whole point of not drinking, isn't it? To make sure you never find out if you like it." I grip the wheel with both hands. I hadn't seen this coming.

"I want to go to parties. I'm a junior now, you know." Charlie puts his hand through his hair.

"I get it. Parties can be fun. But what if you *pretend* to drink?"

"I've thought of that already. It's impossible. The guys will just give me more beers." He leans back and closes his eyes.

He is earnest and lovely, and I want to freeze him like this.

"I'd like you to wait. I think you should wait."

"But I'll be much more respected if I drink."

"But you already *are* respected."

Why is it so important to him? This isn't like him, to want to break the rules. But it's also entirely like him to plan how he'll break the rules.

*PART FOUR*

## *BORDER CROSSINGS*

WE CROSS THE BORDER into Canada easily, and the landscape widens into even more trees, if that's possible. The land feels bigger here. The view more expansive. I'm not sure if this is true, or if it's just that we've left America behind and are somehow relieved.

Charlie falls back to sleep.

I have to pinch my face to stay awake. Joan Jett comes on the radio. When I worked on the videos in London, I did lighting primarily, and some sound. Joan Jett was more beautiful in person than she was on MTV. Though *beautiful* isn't the word I mean. I mean a word that combines strength and beauty.

This part of my life feels odd when I think about it, but it was very natural then, and for a while afterward I just wanted to be like her.

When the videos were done, I traveled to the northern coast of Italy by myself and met a man named Matteo, who drove me into the hills to his stone house, where his friends were eating dinner. They were kind to me, even though it was strange that I had come, and I found out later the friends had dared Matteo to go to the village and find a woman tourist who would agree to a meal with him.

After dinner he drove me back to my hotel in the village and called me Venus de Milo. After Botticelli, he said.

I thought this was funny. I was still so young.

Then he got out of the car and walked me around the natural

pools on the north side of the town where we had to balance on stone walls that separated one pool from the other. He said many people swam there.

I could have fallen into the ocean, or other things could have happened to me. I knew Lara would be mad at me for going with him, and I kept her with me like a witness.

When I thought about Kit, he felt impossibly far away. I didn't know if we'd ever close the distance between us again, and this was okay, because my life was changing. I stayed in the village with Matteo for several weeks before I saw that he was holding on to a false idea of who I was, and then I left.

WHEN CHARLIE WAKES UP, we're about an hour from the hospital, and he says he's so hungry. Could we please stop for food? *Any* food?

I have the impulse I get on car trips to explain everything I feel to the boys—Matteo and loving people with all your heart and daring to leave them to be true to yourself.

I have dangerous amounts of adrenaline because of all the driving, but I know if I tell Charlie about Matteo, he'll say, *Why are you telling me this? What about Dad? Where was Dad during all of this?*

He's often worried about Kit's feelings. In this way Charlie is our emotional accountant as well as moral police.

He tells me that Lucy wants to apply for early decision at Smith College in Massachusetts.

"It's a great school," I say. Even though I had no idea Charlie knew what Smith College was. "What's she writing her college essay about?"

"The life and death of stars. You know she's taking quantum physics, right? You know she's really into it?"

"I did not know. You tell me little."

"Astrophysics and intersectional feminism."

I don't think that he ever used the words *intersectional* and *feminism* together in a sentence before he met Lucy. I try not to smile.

"Maybe I'll apply to colleges in Boston," he says. "She wants me in the same state."

Then the song "Party in the U.S.A." comes on. Miley Cyrus says, "Got my hands up, they're playing my song."

I love this song. And the boys seem to love to make fun of the way I love this song. I don't care. I hold on to the steering wheel with my left hand and wave my right hand in the air above my head.

The DJ played the song at Candy's oldest daughter's wedding in June, before Kit left, and Sam got up in the yard and danced. He's a natural dancer, like his father, and it was the greatest thing to watch him dance again.

I'm not a natural, but I put my hands in the air with Miley Cyrus, and I jumped up and down in the yard with everyone else, and I loved it.

Sam looked embarrassed and stopped dancing and came and took my hands. "Hands down, Mom. Please dance with your hands below your hips."

Charlie stood over by the wedding cake table, laughing at us.

I couldn't stop. I put my hands in the air again.

I think it took several days for Sam to forgive me for this. He might still be forgiving me. There was a girl from his school at the wedding he was trying to impress.

But when the chorus starts up in the car, both boys sing with me. Sam is smiling, and we all have our hands up in the air.

THE HOSPITAL IS IN a residential part of Halifax where the streets are lined with pine trees and one-story wooden houses from the 1970s. The building itself looks more like a brick retirement home than a hospital. When I park in the lot the boys jump out and run inside.

By the time I get to Kit's room they're kneeling by his bed, and he's touching their hair and faces. I try not to cry. Because there he is.

His hair has gotten longer in the week I've been away, and someone should cut it. I will cut it. I should have already done that. The fluorescent lights make his skin look orange.

I've decided to forgive him for the woman with the dog. I know nothing about her, and it's selfish of me to hold on to it.

This is what I think Charlie would say. That I need to get over it and that I should never have left the hospital in the firstplace.

Charlie says I worry too much about Sam and him and that I have to stop and let them grow up.

But when I was up here last week, the boys told me I had to come home, and Sam smoked pot in the McDonald's parking lot. It's confusing to me how I'm not meant to worry.

Sam arm-wrestles Kit on the bed and lets him win.

"You're a tough boy now," Kit says. "Look who's beating you, Mr. LeBron James."

Sam smiles and gives Kit a hug and lets out a little yell, like he's releasing pent-up emotion.

Kit pushes himself up with his hands and hangs his legs over the side of the bed. He's allowed to wear his own sweatpants now. The gray ones. And he's got on the long-sleeved T-shirt with the name of his cousins' lobster house in Lubec on the front.

He looks older today, with the longer hair. A little out of it, honestly.

"How are you feeling today? I mean really. How?"

"Terrible, Jilly." He laughs.

Then the boys laugh too.

"Just look at me. I've got to get out of this place. You have the keys to the Subaru, don't you, Charlie?"

Charlie smiles, and Sam says, "That's why we're here, Dad. To take you home with us."

"All right, then." Kit puts his hand over his heart and taps his chest a few times. "All right."

Then he asks Sam to bring him the walker over by the door.

Sam lunges for it and carries it over.

Kit stands up from the bed using the walker to balance himself. Then he bends over the walker, like he's resting, and we can't really see his face, but I think he's wincing from the pain.

He starts moving slowly toward the green chair, which has been moved to the window since I left.

He uses the walker to help lower himself down, and winces again. I see it this time. He can't hide it.

"Are you really supposed to be doing this?"

"It's better now, Jilly."

He sighs this big sigh I've never heard before, and asks Sam about the basketball team and whether they'll finally beat Sagmore this year.

"How long before you leave?" He seems spacy.

"You mean like leave and go to the hotel?" I ask him. "But we just got here. Remember?" What's he talking about?

Sam pulls one of the white plastic chairs next to Kit and puts his feet up on the windowsill over the heating grate.

Charlie goes into the bathroom and takes a shower, which I can't believe. Since he started dating Lucy he's much more concerned about hygiene, and I'm sure the shower here is better than ours on the island. But right now?

Then Linda, the nurse, comes in and points at Sam. "Is that one of yours, Kit? Is that your baby?" She smiles.

Kit smiles this big grin. "That's Sam, the younger one."

"You came all this way to see your father, didn't you?" she says. "Lucky boys to get to see your father. Lucky father to see the boys."

Last week Linda told me she grew up in Kenya but has lived in Canada since she was eighteen, and she likes it here except for winters and the fact that her mother and father and brother are still in Nairobi.

"I miss them," she said, "like you could not believe."

She puts two fingers on Kit's wrist now to get his pulse. "This is good. This is what we want. Let's keep the number that way."

I follow her out to the hall. "He doesn't seem like himself in there, Linda. What meds is he on today?"

"Percocet." She nods as if she's counting to herself. "Let's see. Yeah, Ambien. Because he wasn't sleeping well this week. He says the pain is bad."

When I go back in the room, both boys are in the plastic chairs by the window, listening to music on their earphones. Kit naps with his right leg extended out from the chair.

Charlie smiles at me and points to his father and does the thumbs-up sign. Then he stares at Kit for another minute, like he's checking to make sure his father's still breathing.

.  .  .

LINDA COMES BACK AN hour later and looks at her watch. Then she puts her hand on Kit's shoulder. "It's that time of day again, Kit."

"Linda." He opens his eyes. "Please don't do this to me."

She points to the door and smiles. "I know you love your physical therapy."

He stands up from the chair using the walker, and seems so wobbly I can't believe we're letting him do this. Linda follows right behind him.

"Come rescue me," he says when he makes it to the door. "If I'm not back in an hour, come rescue me."

He was injured badly only once before. It happened when Sam had just started walking. We took the boys to Wiggins Beach, and Kit decided to swim around Sag Island. It's a thing the locals do. He'd made it around to the back side, where we couldn't see him anymore, when a wind came up.

I'd walked the boys back to the car and strapped them in their car seats and gotten in the driver's seat and closed my eyes. I was often trying to steal little rests from them back then, and I didn't see the woman in the blue windbreaker come up next to the car.

She tapped on my window. "Are you with the swimmer?"

I told her if she meant my husband, then yes.

"Well, it looks bad." She was older, with wrinkled skin around her entire mouth. "The lifeguards are with him, and I've called the fire department."

A wave had picked Kit up and carried him to the rocks near the fort, and at first the doctors thought he'd broken his back. He had to lie in bed that whole month of August. He couldn't fish at all.

I took the burned-tasting Sanka to him in bed, and I wondered how long we could hold on to the trawler.

But he was funny about it. He seemed resigned, or like he even enjoyed it. He wanted to make love in new positions because of his back. It was amazing to have him to myself and not have to share him with the boat.

LINDA PUSHES KIT BACK from physical therapy in a wheelchair, and he has his arms up in the air like he's victorious, but he can't get his breath. I don't know if he knows that I see it, and that I'm watching him.

Sam's lying on the bed with his eyes closed and the earphones in. He's stopped talking, at least for now, about how *beat the state of Maine is* and how he'd like to live in the hospital with Kit and help the nurses do stuff.

He doesn't say which stuff he'll do, and we don't ask.

Linda rolls the wheelchair right up to the side of the bed and Kit leans over and pulls the earphones out of Sam's ears.

Sam screams, and Linda and Kit both crack up.

When Sam sees his father, his face changes.

"Oh, hey. Don't mind me," Kit says. "You're just in my bed."

Sam chooses to smile. Then he climbs out, and Linda helps Kit sit up on the bed and turn himself around and lie down.

"Give me your phone, mate," Kit says to Sam. "I want to see this thing."

I try not to laugh. I tell Linda I finally have some backup on my antiphone campaign.

She shakes her head at us and goes out to the hallway.

"Thanks a lot, Dad. You leave us in Maine with Mom, then you take my phone?" Sam looks over at me and grins.

"Ouch," I say.

"I'm not going to keep it, Sam." Kit raises his eyebrows at me. "I just want to see it."

Sam hands it to him. Then he and Charlie go out to the parking lot to take the Subaru to a gas station for snacks, because they're both *starving*.

"Get me something too," Kit calls to them when they're out in the hall. "Surprise me!"

I'M IN THE GREEN chair over by the window, trying to think of something good to say. I feel an unremitting tiredness. There's a void in the room now that the boys have taken all their energy with them.

Kit asks why they don't want to talk to him anymore.

"What do you mean? They love talking to you. But you have to talk to them about things they want to talk about. They're boys. They're right there waiting for you."

"They don't miss me." He closes his eyes.

It's unlike him to feel this bad for himself.

"They miss you too much. It's not good how much they miss you." I'm not sure he understands what I mean. "They listen to you. They really listen. So please tell Sam not to do drugs." I smile, but my mind starts turning in on itself. "Please tell him."

"I did drugs, and I'm fine." He looks out the window. "Well, I'm not really fine. I've got a trawler I can't use, I'm crippled, and I got pummeled on my quotas this year."

"Please don't say that. Please don't say any of that." I walk over to the bed and take his hand. "Pot is different. It's much stronger. Please talk to him."

"Look at me, Jilly. It's a joke, really. You could say the industry's killing me."

"I'm not listening. You're tired. It's been too much with us here."

"I only ever wanted to make a living like my dad did."

He's still more melancholy. More openly emotional, and I'm trying to understand if he'll stay this way or go back to the way he was before the accident.

"Please don't let the bank take my boat while I'm gone, Jilly. My mother wanted that boat for me. It was her plan."

He doesn't talk about his mother, ever. And the unspoken rule is that no one else can talk about her.

I've always known that what was between them was special. And that because his mother died when he was ten, Kit didn't get some of the things a child needs. He didn't get to understand himself through his mother's eyes for long enough, or to hold on to a story of his family that had her in it alive.

It's rare that after twenty years someone you love surprises you.

I bend down and whisper, "No one's going to take your boat away."

I don't know what we're going to do about the boat. But we'll keep it somehow. We can't sell it.

"Your mother would be proud. Look at the boys you've raised." I've never referred to her this way.

But I've had my own conversations with her in my head. What woman doesn't have conversations with the mother of the man she loves?

I do think she'd be proud of the boys and of the life we've made on her island. But I'll never know. I am hit by a wave of sadness that I'd been able to avoid until then. I have no idea how I'll tell the boys if he can't come home with us. Sadness comes for me in the pale hospital room with the cinder-block walls and concrete floor where I know people before us have suffered.

His eyes are closed and his hair has been pushed back from his face in a way I don't recognize. I'm not sure if he's sleeping or if he'll remember what he's said.

The boys walk back in and break the tension. They're carrying three different brands of Canadian salt-and-vinegar potato chips and want to take the chips down to the common room and watch ESPN on the bigger screen and do a taste test. They're excited about this.

"It's too much," I say. "Too much for Dad. No more walking. All too much."

"Don't listen to your mother," Kit says. And the boys smile and bring the walker back over to the bed and help him stand.

Then they walk with him slowly, slowly down the hall.

I follow behind, trying to leave the sadness back in the hospital room. I can hear Charlie say that we'll get a wider boat to go back and forth to the mainland if Kit needs to use a wheelchair.

"I won't be needing a wheelchair." Kit laughs. "Do you see a wheelchair anywhere near me?"

He sits down on the edge of one of the big, brown armchairs close to the TV and extends his right leg. It doesn't look comfortable. We can't stay here long. The boys sit on the carpet and talk to the TV.

I lean against the wall by the door and am able to speak with the bifocal doctor when he pokes his head in.

I ask him when Kit might be let go. "Is there a chance it could even happen this Sunday?"

He tells me there's a blood infection that seems to be slowing Kit's recovery. "There is no way that your husband will leave with you Sunday," he says. Then he's gone.

I HOLD ON TO the part about the blood infection while the four of us walk back to Kit's room. I don't share it with any of them, so it becomes my secret.

The boys and I pull chairs around Kit's bed and play chess on the tray Kit uses to eat the bad hospital food.

Charlie beats Kit. Then Sam beats Kit.

But Sam refuses to play Charlie for the championship. "Charlie always wins, so what's the use in playing him anyway?"

We switch to Oh Hell. It's Sam's favorite card game.

I think Charlie knows Sam's cheating, but that it's better not to say anything about it.

The stress of the hospital gets to you and plays with your mind. The metal smell and the cinder-block walls and the three watercolors of sailboats on blurry oceans above Kit's bed.

Sam plays a card out of turn. He looks so tired to me now. We need to get to the hotel and sleep.

"Rules, Sam," Charlie says. "Card games have rules for a reason."

Then I say, "Please stop pretending that you're not cheating, Sam."

It's a stupid thing to say, and I regret it immediately. But it takes only one thing to set Sam off.

He stands up and throws his cards in the air and yells, "I hate everything about this family."

Then he runs into the hall. Charlie goes after him.

Kit and I sit in the silence and talk to each other without speaking. We've always done this well.

Something I'm working on is how not to bait Sam, because it's never worth it. I feel I baited him this time, and that it's somehow my fault he's run out of the room. We should have gone to the hotel earlier.

Kit says, "Well, that was a shitshow."

"That," I say, "is basically what we've been dealing with since you left."

When Sam loses control like this, I feel it in my stomach.

Kit says, "I'm trying like hell to get out of here and come home. But now there's an infection, and I swear it feels like I'm never going to leave this place."

I take his hand. "Of course you will get better. Of course you'll come home."

I can sense our hold on things slipping. "You'll come home, and we'll figure things out with the boat. So many people are rooting for you. Shorty wants you back, and I've never seen Jimmy more worried about someone. Sleep." I stand and lean over the bed and kiss him on his face. "You need sleep."

When I see him drift off, I go out to the nurses' station, where Linda and two other nurses are eating homemade pumpkin bread. None of them has seen Sam.

Then I walk down the hall to the elevators and wait for the doors.

Please let the boys be inside.

They each step out holding a green apple and a Hershey bar, and I feel such relief. Maybe I can be absolved of my guilt.

I raise my eyebrows at Charlie, and he raises his back and this is how I know things are going to be okay with his brother.

We walk past the nurses' station, and Linda says she'd like

some of Sam's Hershey bar, and he laughs, like he's always this agreeable.

KIT IS CRYING IN the bed when we get there. It's the most surprising thing.

Jimmy has rules about who's weak and who's strong and who cries. And except when the boys were born, I haven't seen Kit cry.

Charlie starts crying too. I've forgotten the last time I saw Charlie cry. He runs over to Kit's bed, sobbing.

Sam stands in the doorway, watching them. You can tell he's struggling over what to do.

He yells, "Don't cry, Dad! We love you!"

Then he punches the wall and goes and buries his head in Kit's stomach.

The three of them stay like this, while I stand by the door, watching.

WHEN KIT FINALLY FALLS asleep again, the boys
and I gather ourselves and drive to the Best Western. The same
one I stayed in last week, next to a one-story shopping center with
the tanning salon and a Thai restaurant.

Charlie says he's so hungry, even though he just ate a pizza in
the cafeteria. I park and he and Sam walk across the parking lot
to the restaurant, and Charlie gets a beef curry to go.

He brings it inside the lobby, where I'm sitting on one of the
fake velvet chairs by the check-in desk, and he tells me that he's trying to eat healthy now. Fewer calories after dark and more protein.

I can't keep up with his dietary restrictions.

Sam has gotten a bag of sour cream potato chips and a root
beer.

We have two queen beds. The insurance checks pay for almost
half of what we owe the hospital. If I'm not careful, I will hyper-
ventilate over this. Sam grew two inches last summer. It's like we
run a small sneaker store with his feet. I put him in his own bed
because he kicks in his sleep. He crawls under the blankets and
plays a rap song very loudly on his phone while he watches a You-
Tube video of the best NBA three-point shots. The song lyrics go
something like "I want to see you naked on the roof."

"Sam! Turn it off. The words are killing me."

"But you aren't meant to listen to the words, Mom." His face
is in his phone.

I lie down on my side of my bed and close my eyes and wait

for the boys to turn out the lights so I can be alone in my mind. When I was here last week, I met a shockingly handsome man at the breakfast buffet.

I'd found the nuts and brown sugar for my oatmeal in little bowls by the milk dispensary, and the man—his name was Steven—got a plate of pineapple and a plate of scrambled eggs and mixed them together. I said I'd never seen that combination before.

We laughed and went to the same table almost by accident, and he told me about his wife, who was in the hospital for heart surgery.

I had no idea how much I missed talking to an adult. My neck hurt from the drive, and he asked thoughtful questions about it, and it was nice to have someone ask me questions.

I told him how Charlie was like Kit in the sense that he wasn't rash and remembered facts the rest of us forgot, like who in the family was allergic to kiwis. I said Sam depended on me too much and was needier than Charlie.

Then I took a sip of coffee and saw myself for a moment, sitting in the Best Western in Halifax saying personal things about my family. I knew I was lonelier than I thought and that I had to leave the hotel. I made an excuse about forgetting an appointment with a doctor. Then I drove back to Kit and never saw Steven again.

SAM IS UP FIRST the next morning and goes into the little bathroom and announces it's time for a shave.

"But you don't need to," Charlie says from his side of the bed. "There's nothing *to* shave."

"Come look." Sam waves him in. "There's a hair here and a hair here." He points above his lip.

The bathroom is white, and each thing in here—the fake marble sink and the fake marble vanity and even the toilet—looks smaller than the usual size. Charlie gets up and goes and leans over the sink, studying Sam's face in the mirror. "Nope," he says. "There's not enough to shave yet. Don't do it."

I get up too and stand in the doorway, trying to be invisible.

"Look at my underarm, then." Sam puts his bare arm up in the air. "Lots of hair."

There is actual armpit hair.

"Don't rush it." Charlie sounds paternal now, like Kit. "It's coming. It's coming."

These sweet moments arrive when I'm not expecting them. Please let neither of the boys ever grow a day older.

Then they file out of the Best Western bathroom. Their work is done. Their hearts are open. Their day is just beginning.

SATURDAY IS QUIET AT the hospital. Kit sleeps on and off, and the boys and I sit by the window. They do homework. I write grant applications and watch the rain. We're getting used to the routines, and the way the nurses come and go. It's almost peaceful. Even though the sadness is still with me, and I'll have to tell the boys the truth soon about Kit's infection.

We bring in pizza for dinner, and Sam finds *The Bourne Identity* on the AMC channel. The boys and I carry chairs over to Kit's bed and sit around him and watch on the TV above the bed.

SUNDAY STARTS MUCH EARLIER than Saturday. The boys eat egg sandwiches at the cafeteria. By eight o'clock Charlie's talking about getting on the road. He has a precalc test tomorrow he needs to study for.

We still haven't told the boys that Kit isn't coming home. My strategy seems to be to give Sam almost no time to react to the news, though this approach hardly ever works.

Then Marsh walks in and waves.

It's worse to see her this time, but almost just as much of a surprise. I had forgotten her.

She puts her little dog down on the bed and has a defiance about her. Like she dared herself to come here and pierce our family.

I watch Kit take in the dog and take in Marsh. He gives her the private smile that he's given me hundreds of times. The one where he looks right into my eyes.

Then he points at her.

"Boys. Boys, this woman is the one who called the Coast Guard. We have her to thank for my life."

"For your *life?*" Sam gets up out of his chair and stands and waves at her. "Like for saving your *life?*"

"You could say that." Kit smiles.

Marsh rolls her eyes.

"That's cool," Sam says. "That's epic."

"Don't listen to him," Marsh says. She has her hair in a giant, floppy bun on the top of her head.

The boys come take the dog from her and pass it back and forth to each other. They've always wanted a dog, and they talk in baby voices to it and ask why we can't get one just like Maxwell. Why not, Mom? Why not?

I haven't heard these baby voices in a long time, and I try not to laugh.

It starts raining hard out, and we have to talk loudly to hear one another over the sound.

Kit asks Marsh if she wants any of the salt-and-vinegar potato chips.

She shakes her head. "We just came to see you."

Then she smiles the warmest smile at him, which feels like an act of possession. How she's able to make me feel bad just by smiling at my husband isn't clear. I try not to stare too long at her Pretenders T-shirt or her enormous silver belt buckle.

She says I must be going out of my mind in the hospital. "Do you want to get out of here? Like get a coffee or something?"

I want to tell her that I *am* going out of my mind. And it has to do with her being in the room. But I say, "I'd love to get a coffee. I'm tired of being the only member of the female species."

It's nine o'clock in the morning now, and we need to get on the road. But I follow Marsh out to the hall anyway. I don't make eye contact with Charlie, so I can't see if he's glaring at me.

I THOUGHT GETTING A coffee meant going down to the cafeteria. Not driving to her apartment. Charlie's going to kill me. I follow Marsh and the dog out to the parking lot and climb in her truck, because it's too weird to say anything now. We drive for maybe five minutes, with Max in Marsh's lap.

Then she pulls into a lot behind a two-story apartment building and gets out with Max and puts him on the ground. There's a little drugstore on the ground level, and she and Max walk past the glass door to the store and up a set of steep wooden stairs attached to the end of the building. Some of the treads are loose, and the wood gives when I step on them.

When we're almost halfway up, she turns and tells me that Kit was going to fix some of these stairs for her—the ones that were the most rotten, she says. But then he got in the accident.

I don't know if I'm meant to be surprised by this. I feel sleepy. Almost hypnotized or something because what am I doing here? I just nod at her.

There's a futon on the floor inside, and a TV, and a little galley kitchen. I sit on a wooden stool by the fridge, and she hands me a mug of Sanka.

I can't take my eyes off her. She's thin and catlike, with coal-colored eyes and oily skin around her nose. She takes a sip of her coffee, wipes her mouth with her wrist, and points to the sink faucet. "He fixed that. Your husband. A genius. It was always leaking before. No one's ever been as kind to me as him. No one."

It's quiet in the apartment, and my arms have the tingly feeling. I don't know if Marsh has told me about the faucet to prove something to me. I can't be sure.

Maybe she thinks Kit came and fixed things because he wants to save her. He likes to save people. But she'd be mistaken if she thinks she has been singled out.

I look on the walls for a clock but can't find one. Charlie's going to be so mad at me. I finish the coffee. Then I say, "I hate to do this, but I think I better head back. The boys want to get on the road and it's a bad idea to start a trip with them pissed off."

She puts my mug in the sink and says she can't imagine living with teenage boys. "Just the sight of a group of them back in high school gave me the creeps. Boys. They were always so menacing."

I can't tell whether or not to feel insulted. It's really warm in here now, or maybe it's that I hardly got any sleep with Charlie in my bed. Am I supposed to respond to what she said?

She says she can't decide whether to have children or not, because of the commitment.

"The commitment?" I'm confused.

"The biggest commitment of your life, and you can't get out of it." She drains her mug and puts it in the sink.

"I've never thought of it that way. About wanting to get out of it. I mean, once you do it, once you have kids, you're so in. There's no getting out."

"My mother didn't see it that way." She laughs. "Jesus, I can't imagine being that tied down."

"It's definitely that. But it's also this opening up of your heart like you cannot imagine. I'm a different person because of my kids. A better person." I can't believe what is coming out of my mouth. "I'll now stop my small speech on procreation. Sorry. Listen. Everyone's on their own journey. I certainly never planned to have kids."

"Right on." Marsh nods. "I get you."

I'm not sure she gets me.

I tell her I really have to pee.

She points me back toward the other room, with the yin-yang poster above the futon and a mess of blankets on the floor.

The only towel I can find is hanging on the back of the bathroom door over a flannel nightgown with white flowers on it. I feel like I had this nightgown once. I grab the towel and dry my hands and see Kit's Patriots T-shirt hanging under the nightgown. The blue one with the armpit tear from the only game that he's gone to in Foxborough. He and Shorty.

The game was the highlight of his life, he told me once, except for meeting me.

I stand in the little bathroom with the silly movie-star lightbulbs over the sink, and I feel gutted over the shirt. Like something at the center of my life is breaking.

ON THE DRIVE BACK to the hospital I try an experiment where I don't talk. It's been part of my training, so I'm pretty good at it. I don't say anything to Marsh, and wait to see what she'll say back to me.

She says nothing. Then she says, "Damn this rain," and doesn't say anything else.

While Charlie and Sam and I were waiting for Kit on the island, and missing him, and trying not to fall apart, he was going to Marsh's apartment and fixing her faucet.

I feel a rash start on my neck.

When I climb out at the hospital, I give her a half wave.


KIT'S IN THE BED watching some pregame football show. The boys are looking for a vending machine in the basement. I stare at my husband until my face feels like it's got tremors.

Then he says, "I'm so sorry."

What's he apologizing for?

I ask him if he is okay. Really okay.

He says he's sorry he can't go home with us and that the accident woke up something in him.

"What will I do with the rest of my life if I can't fish?" He waves me over to the bed and reaches for my hand. "I've missed you so much."

I say, "I'm having a hard time with this."

"With what?" He keeps holding my hand.

"I don't understand the woman who comes here with her dog."

"You mean Marsh?"

"That's who."

"I'm helping her."

"Helping her with what?"

"She's someone who's suffered. She's a friend."

"How?"

"How what?"

"How has she suffered? Your shirt's in her bathroom." I keep looking to see what his face is doing, then I look away.

"What shirt?" He sits up more in the bed.

"The one under her nightgown in her bathroom."

We've never had anything close to this between us. I walk over to the window and stare at the birch trees and feel frozen in the dread. He's slept with her. He must have.

He says, "I can't believe how you're treating me right now."

I don't think he understands anything about me. How rigid with fear I am. "Tell me you haven't gone to her apartment."

"We have days off the boat, Jilly. I help her with the dog."

"You help with the dog. I lie to you about what it's like on the island so you don't know how bad it is there."

"You get to be with our children. Is it really that bad?"

I pretend I haven't heard him.

"I mean, who is she? And if you're sleeping with her, I'll never forgive you. You should never ask."

"You're mad." He stares at me.

I want to hit something like Sam did yesterday.

"No, you're crazy," he says. "What are you talking about? Your forgiveness?"

I know fishermen who go on long trips to fish in other waters because it eases their marriage, and because their marriage is dying. But that wasn't us.

"I think she's in love with you."

The prickly feeling goes up and down my legs. There's something between them. I saw it.

"You're out of control."

"That's what Sam says to me whenever he's guilty." I'm giving him a chance to tell me the truth. I've heard about these moments in a marriage. This one clear moment where everything in the past turns.

"Jesus, Jilly. You're wrong."

"It's simple, Kit." I try to slow my way of speaking. "Tell me if you slept with her."

He stares out the window. "I don't understand you. I've been up here for weeks fishing for you."

I feel something frantic inside. "Yes or no, Kit?"

"You left me here. I don't get it. I wouldn't have left."

This is all I need to know—this fact that he can't answer me. Jesus.

The room feels alien and too warm now. There's the sanitized, metallic smell. I hear myself say, "We have children. One of them was smoking pot. I have a film to finish." I'm so angry at him for trying to put the blame on me. "We can't make payments on the trawler. We can't make any payments."

"We're waiting. It's a waiting game here. I make a friend, and you won't give me this."

"Did you have a sleepover with your friend?"

The door is slightly open to the hall and people walk back and forth and call to one another, and nurses and orderlies push patients by in wheelchairs and on gurneys. While inside our little room, I'm shuddering.

"Marsh knows boats. She understands."

He looks like my husband, but who is he?

"She understands what, Kit? I moved to the island and gave up everything for you."

This last part's untrue. I say it anyway and try not to raise my voice, but it catches and gets ragged at the end. I swallow a sob. He will not see me cry.

"You made me come here. You said we needed money."

"We need money, but I never said that I wanted you to go." I shake my head. "Maybe I've never known you." I walk to the door.

"You've always known me. I'm not complicated. She's a friend."

Leave now. Get out of the room. I stand by the door and search for one last thing that would reach him and mean something. He's always been fair. Always been generous. "Why did you need a friend?"

"We all do."

I go out to the hall and want to lie down on the floor and close my eyes and scream. But the boys come upstairs with little bags of pretzels and Cokes and go into Kit's room and give him high-fives.

"Let's hug it out," Kit says to them.

"Mom," Sam yells to me in the hall. "Mom, please get in here. We need you."

I have to go in and put my hand on Sam's shoulder. I'm meant to hold Kit's hand with my other hand so that we make a circle, but I can't do it. I just can't.

Sam asks why Kit's still in bed if he's coming home with us. "You're not even packed, Dad."

"I can't come with you today, mate. I can't. The doctors say I need more time here. Maybe a week."

"What are you even *talking* about?" Sam says. "That's why we came. *To get you.*"

Then he starts crying, which he never does, and we're all

thrown. It's good to see him cry, even though I think he's ashamed by it. I still believe it's good.

Then he starts kicking the heating grate under the window-sill. Kicking it and kicking it.

"Stop it," I say. "Stop it right now."

He cries harder.

"It will be all right, mate," Kit says. "It will really be all right. Come hug it out with me."

Sam walks back over to the bed and puts his face in Kit's chest.

I can't look at them. I have to get out of the hospital. I go wait in the parking lot.

CHARLIE'S LYING DOWN IN the back of the Subaru, and I'm standing by the driver's-side door while Sam and Linda have a moment in the parking lot.

It's eleven in the morning and Sam believes he could stay in Nova Scotia and sleep in the armchair in Kit's room.

Linda's talking him down.

The leaves on the trees out here have turned many shades of orange and red and fallen to the ground, so the hospital seems even lonelier than it did when we got here.

Linda puts her hand on Sam's arm and says she never lets patients leave her care when they're fighting an infection. "You've got to believe me on this," she says, like she's trusting him with her confidence.

Sam wipes his eyes again and says his dad doesn't *look* sick to him, so why can't he come with us? He thinks it's a conspiracy to keep his father away from him.

Linda says, "Lots of people who don't look sick are sick. You need to go now."

She points at me and we lock eyes for a second. Then I look away. I don't want Sam to think I'm staring at him.

Charlie's moaning in the back about the precalc test.

"Your mother is waiting," Linda says. "You've got school, and I've got your dad covered here."

Sam finally gives up and gets in the car, but he refuses to sit in front with me.

"Once again," he says after he puts his seat belt on in the back, "Jillian has lied. Once again Jillian has not told the truth."

I don't even try to answer this.

It's my fault Kit has the infection. My fault Kit had the accident.

"What will we do without Dad?" Sam says. "What will we do? What will we do?" He stares at me in the rearview mirror.

I REMEMBER THE TIME Kit came home after a fishing trip and found me leaning against the fridge with my eyes closed. It was two in the afternoon, and I'd just gotten the boys to sleep. They were three and four years old, and I hadn't changed my clothes in a couple days. I didn't think I'd ever change my clothes again, because I had two little boys with penises camping out in my head, and I lived on an island in Maine and never saw other humans.

I told Kit it was a mistake.

"What was?" he whispered, because the boys were sleeping on the wooden seats he'd built under the window in the living room. We had to whisper all the time when the boys were sleeping.

"To live out here."

"What are you talking about?"

"On the island."

He came and put his arms around me, and I felt like I was standing above my body. I hadn't begun shooting the Harwich film yet, and Kit was someone who had a job on his boat and left the island for days while I rarely left. I could see him as a separate person. This didn't happen often, that he was separate from me.

This is how it feels in the car. That he's separate from me again.

The boys nap, and I keep looking back in the rearview mirror at their greasy hair and their long, smooth necks.

Kit broke his nose once when a winch hit his face, and they had to bandage it and keep fishing because they were four days out. His nose has a small rise that skews it and makes it different from Charlie's and Sam's.

They wake up an hour later and start playing a game called Clash Royale on their phones, which I think involves gnomes.

Sam asks Charlie if he's kissed Lucy.

Charlie tells Sam to please shut up.

Charlie seems older to me after the hospital. He was so good with Kit and with the nurses. Both boys were.

Marsh is someone who seems hungry and also vain. I want to warn the boys about this dangerous combination. Then I can't decide if I've made the whole thing up.

WE CROSS BACK INTO America, and it's so easy again. The blond boy in the back has a clueless smile, and the rule-abiding, darker-haired one hands his passport over to the immigration officer before it's asked for.

After we're through, Charlie says it took Lucy and her family three years to get visas to fly from their refugee camp near Nairobi to Atlanta. Her father still doesn't have his visa. Lucy hasn't seen him in three years.

Sam says, "That's *terrible*."

Charlie puts his feet between the seats. "You have no idea how much Lucy misses him. It's bad at night. Really bad. Like it worries me. They're not sure when he can ever come."

"Jesus," Sam says. "I mean, *Jesus*."

"It's been years," Charlie says. "Years. They're like completely powerless."

We're quiet after that. All of us thinking.

At least I think that we're thinking.

CHARLIE WAKES UP IN the backseat and asks if either of us knows what determines a star's color.

I'm looking for a place to get a milk shake. I've been looking for the last half hour.

"No, Charlie, I do not know what determines a star's color."

"Well, the surface temperature for starters, Mom."

"You're weird," Sam says. "You talk so much about galaxies and shit."

Charlie says, "Jesus, you're always on me, Sam."

WE GET TO BANGOR, and Charlie closes his eyes again.

Then Sam climbs up front and tells me he doesn't miss Dad at night at home if he's the first one asleep, so every day he tries to get really tired.

"If I can't fall asleep, I worry."

"I'm so, so sorry," I say. "I'm sorry it makes you worry."

The last thing Sam needs is more worry.

He says, "Did you know that when people drink they change their behavior?"

We're in the tundra of trees now, and the adrenaline isn't working anymore. There are too many things happening at once. I can't drive and keep up.

"I did know that. Tell me more." I never thought my life

would hinge on the confessions of an exhausted teenager. But the stakes feel high with him.

"Like when a group of guys drink alcohol, they do things they wouldn't normally do, like run around in the snow or dance. I think I'll probably have to try it."

"You will?"

"I will." He looks straight ahead at the road. "Or maybe I'll be the designated driver." He pauses.

"But that will get old. Let's not have any drunk people in your car. You or anyone else, okay?" I am trying to keep him talking.

"Yeah. Dealing with drunk people in my car would be beat."

"Very beat."

Whenever he's talking, it's good. "And here's the thing," I say. "You're sixteen. Underage drinking is illegal, and you signed the contract to be on the basketball team."

"Okay, Mom. I get it. I get it. I was just trying to have a *conversation* with you."

Now I've ruined it.

He turns on the radio, and Charlie wakes up angry about the noise.

I tell them there's amnesty if either of them gets into trouble and needs to call me. They can call day or night and I'll come. No questions. But if I find out they're doing drugs, there will be such consequences.

Sam rolls his eyes at me. "I don't understand what real kids do. How do they not get crucified by their parents like me?"

"You're a real kid," Charlie says.

"We have not crucified you yet," I say. "Do you feel crucified, Sam?"

Then I tell them how the man I met in Italy did lots of drugs, and this was partly why I left him. "I think he was punishing himself for something he couldn't articulate. I could never figure out what it was."

"You just *left him?*" Sam says. "Jesus, Mom."

"I think this is called oversharing," Charlie says. "We need to call Dad. Does Dad even know this stuff? Why are you telling us this?"

"It's life, Charlie," I say. "It's real life. It is what drugs can do to you. It's what we call cautionary. It's about not always trusting the people who you think love you."

"Cautionary? It's *freaky,*" Sam says.

"I knew I'd find love with your father. I knew it."

"Earth to Dad," Sam says. "Come in, please. Mom's totally losing it."

Charlie stares at me in the rearview as if he entirely disapproves. As if these new facts have physically changed who I am to him. But I'm the same person, driving them back to our island.

I TAKE CHARLIE TO Lucy's house. Because even though I'm kind of delirious from driving, I promised him I would. I believe you have to live up to at least half your promises if you want to have any credibility left with teenagers.

Lucy lives on one of the side streets near Tugboat Pizza. Charlie runs toward her front door with his backpack and doesn't turn around once to wave at us. I drive away, and my thoughts go to depressing, dead-end places. Charlie leaving me. Charlie growing up. Who will I be without Charlie?

I imagine a different life and a different marriage. Maybe Austin, Texas. A bakery with some sun.

"Please tell me you're not crying," Sam says. "Please say you're not."

I wipe my tears with my hand.

He says, "I need to get away from this family and all the crying soon. I need to get the band to Vermont."

I take a left onto the bridge. "It will be good of you to wait until your father gets home." I do not even try to hold back on my sarcasm.

Sam has no facial expression while we cross the bridge. It feels like he's shutting down. When we've made it to the other side, he says he's so hungry he's going to faint.

I stop at Dairy Queen because there's nowhere else to go. He devours a hamburger and a large fry in the car, and the food seems to restore his anger. He says he can't believe how far Sewall is from Nova Scotia. Then he stops talking to me.



IT'S FREEZING IN THE house, even after I light the woodstove. We can't stay on the island anymore. It's been a mistake to try to stay. I make us cheese omelets, and we eat them on the rug in front of the stove in silence.

Everything I do in the house feels unnatural now. Everything I say to Sam feels portentous. Like he *knows* that Kit left his shirt in Marsh's apartment and that our lives have been thrown into disbelief, but he's not saying.

Then I remember Sam doesn't know anything and that Kit and I are the adults and Sam's counting on us.

The moon is full and blue, and the water and trees are also a little blue. Sam still won't talk to me. It's like being in the house by myself, except for his passive aggression, which feels like another person because his passive aggression is that big.

He finally goes upstairs.

But I have to wait for Charlie, who doesn't come back until almost nine. I'm beside myself by then.

I watch from the window while he ties the rowboat up at the dock.

"Where have you been?" I ask when he comes in.

He looks confused by the question. "You know where I've been."

He sits on the rug by the stove and takes his sneakers off. "Why are you asking me this?"

"Because it's late and cold and dark out. I never thought you'd be so late."

"We had studying to do. When did nine become late?"

"On Sunday nights on the island in November, nine is late. You have school tomorrow." I can't understand it.

Lara keeps reminding me how great it is that Charlie's in a relationship, and that it's much better for his soul than hooking up so I'm meant to encourage the relationship. She keeps threatening to explain what hooking up really means, but I don't want to know.

PART FIVE

# DO YOU KNOW
# HOW MUCH I LOVE YOU?

A STORM HITS IN the night, and the ocean sounds like thousands of pieces of glass breaking on the rocks. The trees bend over on themselves, and the windows bang on the casings. They'll shatter, or the patched roof will fly off, but I feel very little about any of it. My husband appears to have been sleeping with a woman who wears a Pretenders T-shirt similar to the one I used to wear circa 1995.

Storms used to be something that Kit and I made it through together. We'd climb in bed after the boys had gone to sleep and look out at the night sky through the window and pray the boats didn't break away. There was nothing else we could do at that hour. We just held hands and waited. Sometimes we made love. I liked it so much when Kit was in our bed with me during the storms and not at sea.


CHARLIE GETS UP AT six and says he can't stop worrying about the boats. He looks thin and muscular, like a younger version of Jimmy. We stand together in the window and watch while the float gets sucked in on the swells. Then pulled back again. Over and over.

The water is higher than I've ever seen it. I don't think the chains on the float will hold. But if the float breaks off, it will take the boats and maybe the ramp with it.

Charlie finally goes back up to bed, because there's nothing we can do but wait. It's a completely helpless feeling. You want to do something. You want to go outside and physically do something, anything, but you can't stop the weather.

I sit on the couch and listen to the wind. We could never make it back across the channel now in any kind of boat. We might as well be on Kit's trawler riding the storm out to sea.

Kit's shirt is in a bathroom in Nova Scotia, and this has broken through something for me. I'd thought of marriage as two people who know each other entirely and will always know each other. But what if they're just two people who share an idea of what life could be, and then one of them changes their idea.

WHEN I WAKE UP the next time, I'm facedown on the couch, freezing. The storm has passed, and there's a pale, pinkish light under the torn clouds.

Sam is in my face. "It's gone, Mom! The float is gone!"

"Oh God." I open my eyes. "I knew it."

The float has never broken off before, because the water has never come so far up.

We all walk outside in our boots and coats and stand at the top of the ramp. The island's covered in snow, and a layer of silvery ice has formed along the shore. The float is gone, and it's not possible to say that everything will be okay. My longing for Kit is sharp and clear.

The boys walk back up to the house and pull the canoe out from under the pine trees and carry it down to the rocks. The water's flat and inky black—the kind of cold you can't survive in for longer than a minute. I watch them paddle out into the channel until I can't see the outlines of their shoulders anymore.

"Come back safely," I say out loud. "Please come back safe." My breath condenses around my face. It will be colder today than yesterday. I can already tell. I turn back toward the house and go begin packing. We need to leave the island before it becomes a prison.

THEY FIND THE FLOAT down in Miller Cove, wedged into an opening in the rocks. Jimmy comes and tows it in front of the house and anchors it. Then he and the boys drill new holes in it and secure it to the rocks with more bolts and chains and ropes.

It takes hours. They walk up to the house afterward. At first Jimmy won't accept anything I offer him. He finally agrees to a coffee with me at the table. He's wearing the blue flannel shirt and dark Wranglers I think he has worn every day I've known him, and he tells us that it is the wrong season to be on the island.

"But we're fine, Jimmy," Sam says. He's changed back into his pajamas and is sitting in front of the woodstove, shivering. "We can't just *leave*. Dad won't want us to do that."

"We're not fine." I look over at Jimmy.

"You're so not fine, Sam," Charlie says from underneath both of the Patriots blankets on the couch.

It's thrown me off to have Jimmy in here. He stops down at the dock to grab Kit or one of the boys, or to loan us some piece of equipment, but he never comes inside. It was Martha's favorite place, and Candy says it makes Jimmy too sad to be in here.

"We're lucky," I tell Sam, "that school got canceled today, but we need to get to the mainland. Even Dad doesn't want us out here anymore, honey."

"Mom, please, *please* don't call me honey. Just call me Sam."

I smile a fake smile. I don't have any more fight left in me.

Charlie says, "We're freezing our butts off here, Sam."

"Why can't we have a house like Robbie does?" Sam says. "Why can't we have an electronic gate and a sauna?"

"We can't have a sauna because we can't afford a sauna." I finish my coffee and glare at Sam. It's embarrassing when he acts like this. Jimmy's the last person you want to be bratty around. It's almost like Sam does it on purpose. I'm sure he does it on purpose.

Charlie looks hard at his brother. "Did you really just need her to explain that to you?"

"Go pack your things, boys." Jimmy stands and pulls his Wranglers up. "I'm taking you all home in my boat."

THE HOUSE IS A wooden A-frame at the top of the hill. It smells like mothballs and old Marlboros, and it's the house that Kit's mother died in. Jimmy could have sold it and bought other, bigger houses in the village during the best lobster years but he didn't. I sleep in Candy's old room with the queen-sized waterbed, left over from Jimmy's last girlfriend, who decided Maine was too cold. Lara and I are watching *Dirty Dancing* on Netflix.

It's late on Thursday afternoon, and she has the laptop balanced on her stomach. I know she's trying to trick me with the movie, so that later I'll agree to get out of bed and go to Sam's basketball team dinner. I've been lying in here most of the week.

When Lara and I were waitresses at the lodge that summer, she dated a lifeguard named Luke Hennessy, who got a scholarship to an acting school in North Carolina. It was almost a cliché, he was so good-looking. So we called him Patrick Swayze.

I blow my nose into a tissue and say he's unrecognizable.

"Who is?" Lara's wearing Sam's blue Avery High sweatshirt because it's so cold in here. I'm not sure Jimmy believes in heat. She takes another potato chip from the bag and points at the screen. "Patrick Swayze?"

"No. The man known formerly as my husband."

"Kit is the same person, Jill. He just left a shirt in a bathroom. Big deal." She thinks I'm overdoing it about the shirt.

"Please." I put my hand out for more chips. She gives me three, which seems stingy. "It is a big deal."

I don't want to get in another argument with her about how it matters when you're married to someone. She never understands. Or she understands, but she doesn't agree and doesn't think the state should have anything to do with the people you love.

"He's a good person," Lara says. "He just left his shirt."

"You can't do that." I stare at the movie. "You can't go over to a woman's house and leave a shirt."

"But you can. Of course you can. And you can be forgiven, because you have a wife and two teenagers. You need to get over it. I don't see what the big flipping deal is."

"It's a deal, Lara. If you lecture me about marriage again, I'll dump that bag of potato chips on your head. He slept with her."

"You don't know that."

"But I do. And you do too. He wouldn't answer me when I asked. He couldn't answer."

My phone rings again.

"You have to pick it up." She grabs my phone off the blanket, before I can, and the computer falls off her lap.

"I don't have to do anything."

"No, you have to. He's in a hospital. Just answer it. I'm trying to save your marriage." She hands me the phone and climbs out of the bed and goes out into the hall. This isn't a joke. Why is she laughing?

Kit asks me about the storm, and if the ramp broke off when the float did.

I think he already knows the answers to these questions.

Then he says, "Why didn't you call me?"

"I didn't need to call you. Your father's been helpful." I stare at the old poster of Linda Ronstadt on the wall above Candy's white bureau and decide to make this as hard for him as possible.

"Where are the boys?"

"Sam's down with Shorty, helping fix up a boat. Charlie's with Candy, stocking shelves."

"Are you going to really talk to me or not?"

"I'm talking to you. This is me talking to you."

"Jilly, don't do this."

"Don't do what?" I refuse to make this about me.

Does Lara ever feel this lonely? Or maybe only married people feel this way.

"God, you're stubborn. I've never met anyone who can hold a grudge the way you do."

"You think this is about holding a grudge? Marriage is trust, Kit. That's what it is."

"I realize I have choices, and I chose poorly, and I'm sorry. I'm really sorry."

"So you slept with her?" My stomach turns over and then it does it again.

There's a silence after this.

"I didn't sleep with her. I went over to help with the dog. It was late. I was tired. It's not what you think. She's a friend. I needed one. It's not easy up here."

But why didn't he need me?

The sky is a punishing, gorgeous blue, and the sun looks like a golden flower.

"I thought I was your friend. I wouldn't lie down with someone in a bed because I was tired. I would never do that to you."

Then I hang up on him.

Lara opens the door. "Did you really just hang up? I can't believe you did that."

She looks kind of possessed, standing by the side of the bed in Sam's sweatshirt with her pale, wavy hair falling down her shoulders.

"I can't believe you were listening."

"Of course I was listening."

"I hung up because he slept with her."

"He slept next to her."

"It's like having sex without the sex." I close my eyes.

"It's not like that at all."

"It's like sex of the mind or something."

"Oh my God, Jill, there's no such thing."

I try to sit up fully in the bed, but it's hard with all the water moving around.

"He's either had an affair or almost had an affair. And you know that, Lara."

It's the thing I think about the most. You say the word *affair,* and it's supposed to hold everything. Like one word can ever explain someone's desperation, when there are hundreds of thousands of molecules spinning inside that word. This is what Charlie taught me. Molecules. Moving at rapid speeds.

Kit either had an affair or almost had one. Lara doesn't talk about how much this hurts. There's no need to. But I can't get distance on it, which is what scares me. It feels out of my control.

"It's not really about the shirt in the end," I say. "I mean, it is. But it's really not. It's that he cares about her."

"We all care about people." She reaches out her arm to me. "We all need different people. It's only normal. It's what people do."

"It would have been his secret." I do not take her hand. "He would have kept it to himself if I hadn't gone to her apartment. That's what I can't forget."

"You don't know that. You don't know what Kit would have done. Maybe we don't need to know all of each other's secrets. I mean, he loves you. A lot of people are looking for connection and not finding it. Please don't ruin everything. Please." She sits down on the side of the bed.

"My husband may be in love with a woman who wears a Pretenders T-shirt and has the largest silver belt buckle I've ever seen."

"He's not in love."

"But how would you know, Lara? How would you really know?"

"Because he's in love with you. I've seen it. You married people don't understand how you give yourselves away. You pretend it's private to be in your marriage, but we can all see. Get up. We're going to get you dressed. You have a basketball team potluck to go to."

THE ONLY THING SAM says to me on the drive to the gym is to please get Dad home. *"Please. Please."*

I end up cornered by the food table with the mother of Derrick, who plays shooting guard. I can't recall her name, but I should know it. She's just come from the Avery hospital where she's an ER nurse.

I tell her that I'm looking forward to the first game.

She says, "Yeah, IDK."

I *think* IDK means "I don't know," but I'm not completely sure.

I say, "It's going to be a fun season. LOL." I smile and hope what I said was okay.

Then Sam materializes next to me. "Mom, can I talk to you for a minute?" He takes my arm and leads me back out to the hall where the two bathrooms are. "You can't talk like that."

"Like what?"

"In text."

He looks older and handsome with the hair pushed out of his eyes. He likes this team so much, and it's good for him. The running around and the bonding.

"Okay. Okay." It's easy to agree, because I don't have any more text to talk in. I don't know any more text.

I want to say I'm sorry any of this is happening, and that I'm only here to support him. That's all I'm here to do. I've been trying to hold him up and am apparently giving my husband only my crumbs.

. . .

WHEN WE GET HOME, I go back to the waterbed. Lara's made spaghetti while we've been gone, and she and Charlie and Jimmy finish eating in the kitchen.

"Please feel my forehead," I ask her when she comes up to check on me. "It's warm, right? I'm sure I have a fever."

She puts her hand on my face. "No fever."

She is kind and does not say how neurotic she thinks I'm being. Then she goes downstairs to help Jimmy clean up.

"REMEMBER WHEN WE HAD power?" I said once to Lara when the boys were babies and I'd escaped to Portland.

"If you mean sexual power, we never had any. None. It just felt like we did."

We were drinking beers down on the pier, and a painting of hers had just been in the museum's biennial. Her career was happening while mine felt stalled.

She wanted to get another beer, but I said I had to drive back to the island.

"It amazes me how much you've changed. It's just a beer. No one's going to die at home while you sit here."

"I have a *family*," I told her. I was so dramatic that it's cringy now.

"There's a world going on out here, Jill. Not everyone wants to move to an island and make babies."

It was one of our few fights. I couldn't tell if she was envious of me for having the boys or if she was mocking me, or both.

"You make it sound elitist or something," I said.

"Well, mothers can totally be that way."

"I can't believe you," I said. "You make it seem like an entirely different thing than it is."

"I'm just saying you're removed up there." She finished her beer.

"Where do you want me to live? My husband fishes, Lara. That's what he does. I have children to raise."

Motherhood had given me somewhere to put all the love I felt inside me. I hadn't known I'd been looking for a place to put all the love. This was what I wanted to say to Lara. But I don't think she wanted to hear it. It was something I kept from my closest friend.

SAM COMES IN NOW and lies next to me in the bed, which I can't really believe.

"Careful," I tell him. "You could make a wave big enough to throw me off the bed."

He laughs.

Sometimes that's all I need from him. I'm getting sleepy. "To what do I owe this visit?"

"It's weird," he says, "to live in Dad's old house without Dad, isn't it?"

"But it's not forever." I can't tell where this is going, but Sam always has a motive. "Tell me how it's weird."

"Because Jimmy's here, and he's never usually here when we are. It makes me think about how everything's different now, and Dad is like really *not here.*"

I take a good look at him. His face is thinner than last week. Is he eating? I try to keep track, but for all I know he could be having Doritos and Coke for lunch every day at school.

"The thing about Jimmy is that you have to humor him. He's

worried, you know. He's Dad's father and he has a problem with people getting sick."

Kit's like this too. If one of the boys even gets a cold, it sets Kit off. Then he's checking temperatures and making them soup. It is the only time he won't go out fishing. I get it. I get that this worry is his mother's legacy. But I don't think Kit sees it. I'm not a therapist, and if I tried to talk to him about it, he'd never listen.

"You okay?" I nudge Sam with my shoulder.

He doesn't push me away. So I put my hand on his face and rub his forehead.

"You miss Dad."

"Of course."

"You wish he was here."

Sam closes his eyes.

"Oh honey, it's okay. It's really all okay."

Tears leak down his gaunt cheeks.

"But it's not okay, Mom. I just *really* worry about him. I like think about Dad all the time, and then I can't sleep. Like what's going to happen to him? When will he be back? I mean, don't *lie* to me again."

"It's not like that at all. Dad's coming home soon, and you're going to bed because you have school tomorrow." I'm losing him. He needs more than words. Or more than my words. I'm not enough.

Lara comes up then and takes Sam's sweatshirt off and tosses it to him.

"Don't leave us," I tell her, and smile, but it's a fake smile.

"You've got this." She looks at Sam. "Your mother has this, right, Sam?"

"I hope so." He climbs out of bed and walks down the hall to his room, and I know I've lost him.

"I have to teach tomorrow," Lara says. "A class of twenty-year-olds on cultural appropriation in abstract art."

"I think Marsh has appropriated my husband."

"I think you need to sleep."

I climb out of the bed and hug her hard. I really don't want her to go, but I say, "Thank you thank you thank you for coming. It means everything."

THERE'S A BASKETBALL SCRIMMAGE on Wednesday night at the Y, where one half of Sam's team is playing the other half, and Charlie and I go because Sam asks us to. He so rarely asks us. He always asked Kit. But I think he's nervous tonight.

The gym at the Avery Y was built underground, and it has no windows and smells of body odor and decades of old sneakers. Sound echoes so it's hard to think. It feels now like this life I'm leading is Kit's life. That he chose it.

His Y. His fishing village. How did this happen? I want to drive up to the hospital and get a look at his face. It would be better if I could see him. I'm going up there tomorrow. I have to.

One half of the team's done something wrong with a play they're meant to run, and the coach yells and bangs his fist on one of the metal chairs.

He gets more worked up as the scrimmage goes on, and then he throws a chair against the cement wall.

I'm embarrassed to be in the gym. I look over at Charlie next to me. "You can't make this stuff up."

He says everything about this coach is ridiculous. "Who would ever *do that*? I mean, throwing a chair in a *scrimmage*."

I FOLLOW HIM TO the dark little lobby at halftime and buy a bag of popcorn and watch him drape his arm over the shoulder of a girl by the vending machines. Then he presses his lips into her hair. I can't stop staring. He's smiling at the girl and nodding while she talks to him. Then he helps her put on a purple parka.

I think he's used some of the new hair gel, so his hair isn't as wavy around his face, and he's wearing the V-neck sweater I bought at Target two years ago that I'd forgotten about.

"Mom." He's got a *please don't ruin this for me* look. "Now you get to meet Lucy."

"Finally!"

I'm sure I overdo it here. I can't help myself.

"She's hungry," Charlie says, and looks at Lucy's face again. "So we're going to go get some food for her at the Tugboat."

"I'm not *so* hungry that I need to be rude, Charlie." She smiles and puts out her hand to me. Her hair sits in loose curls around her face. She has on jeans and a cool red sweater with a blue heart on it and patent leather ankle boots with a chunky heel that make her almost as tall as Charlie. Her skin is a deep brown color, and her eyes seem to take in everything—my hair, my old jeans, my big amoeba coat. "Hello, Mrs. Archer, so good to finally meet you."

"Oh no, it's so good for me to meet *you.* I've heard so much. We have to get you down to the house. We have to, Charlie, don't we?"

Charlie says we do. But he's got the faraway look and keeps walking with her toward the door.

"Have fun." Without thinking I add, "You know how much, right?"

He turns and shoots me a look that says, *Don't ever say that again.*

I get myself together and tell him to have a great time. Then I stand in the lobby and suck in my breath.

Well, that wasn't good. That didn't go well at all.

I eat more of the popcorn and walk back into the gym alone.

WHEN THE SCRIMMAGE IS over, I back the car out of the Y parking lot carefully, carefully.

Charlie's in love. I've seen it.

Sam's changed out of his uniform, but he's still sweaty and worked up. I ask him if it bothers him when his coach throws chairs.

"Coach told us when he throws chairs and swears at us, it's because he *likes us,* Mom. *He cares about us.*"

"That's bullshit."

*"Excuse me?"*

"That's a bad excuse to get to yell at a bunch of boys."

"You don't understand."

"No, I understand perfectly well."

"No, you weren't there, okay? You *think* you understand. But Coach is trying to get us to *win.* He says he just wants us to live up to our potential, Mom."

"Throwing a chair is a strange way to show you care about people."

Then Sam pulls his protective membrane down, so there's no way for me to get in.

He almost stopped playing basketball a few years ago because of the coaches who liked to humiliate boys and yell at them. It was the strangest, cruelest thing, how these men acted.

Once when Sam was ten, we took him to a different gym with a different coach in a town farther away. Kit set it up through a friend from high school, but I had to take Sam to the first practice, because Kit wasn't back from fishing. The coach was famous for his punishments, and he yelled at the boys and called them girls and pussies and told them they were weak.

Near the end of the practice, he made two of the youngest boys do twenty push-ups while all the other boys watched, and I was pretty certain he was going to punish Sam next for something he'd done wrong. But the practice ended without more punishment. Sam walked outside and leaned his head on the roof of our car and sobbed. It was dark out, and no one could see him but me. I told him that we were never going back there and we didn't.

SAM'S INSTAGRAM POST TONIGHT: a series of direct-to-the-camera monologues by famous professional athletes who've lost their fathers and say they've never given up.

ON SATURDAY MORNING I'M floating on the water-
bed, and I can see her kitchen again in my mind: the faucet and
shallow sink you can't fit a dinner plate in. The two-burner stove
and loneliness and chemical smell. I don't know if the smell came
from what Marsh cleaned with or from the pharmacy down
below. I wanted to get out of there even before I saw his shirt in
the bathroom.

Most of the time I think people want connection and don't
know how to ask for it. Marsh did not want connection with me. I
knew this as soon as she gave me the Sanka. She wanted my husband. With me she was just collecting facts.

I don't drive up to see Kit. Instead I do something I haven't
done in months. I fall back asleep.

When I go downstairs in my sweatpants it's almost noon, and
Jimmy's at the stove frying bacon. Sam's at the kitchen table doing
an art project he says he hates.

"What is this thing you hate so much, Sam?" Jimmy asks.
He seems smaller today in the Wranglers, if that's possible. As if
he aged in his sleep.

"My life map." Sam's got a piece of white poster board on the
table, and three Magic Markers, and a bottle of Elmer's Glue, and
a small pile of family photos I found for him last night. He looks
desperate.

"What in hell is a life map?" Jimmy says.

"Think of a family tree." I pour my first cup of coffee. I'm glad for both of them this morning and how they distract me.

There's a photo of Jimmy and Martha on the wall above Sam's head taken before Kit was born. Maybe 1972. They're sitting on the stern of their first lobster boat. Martha has her hair tucked into a plaid kerchief and is wearing tan polyester slacks with no pockets. I've stared and stared at this photo over the years, looking for clues to her.

People say she was a force of good in the village and also at the phone company where she worked for seventeen years. She had the same crinkly eyes as Kit, and the same chiseled nose, and the same smiling mouth that hid her stubbornness.

In all the time I've known Jimmy, I've never seen him hug anyone. But there he is with his arm across Martha's shoulders. I look at the photo. Then I look over at Jimmy cooking his bacon. And all I see now is his heartbreak. If you read this house carefully, that's what you always see.

Jimmy comes over to the table and stares at Sam's poster. "Looks to me like you're almost done here."

Kit can't recall a day when Jimmy helped him with his homework. Jimmy was always on his boat. Now he is what he calls semiretired. He turns the burner off and sits down on the other side of Sam with the bacon.

I'm slightly more afraid of him than usual. He keeps giving me his disapproving look. Like if he could find the right time, he'd openly criticize me for not going back to the hospital, or say something about the way I've let Sam grow his hair long, which would be another way of saying *Why in God's name are you not at the hospital?*

I think Candy's also wondering about me. She keeps saying she and Flip will take the boys so I can go be with Kit, and I keep telling her that she doesn't have to. But I don't know how much longer I can punish him.

Sam has drawn a simple brown tree on the poster board, and on each leaf of the tree he's written the name of a family member. Kit and Jimmy and Candy and Charlie and me.

I stare at the tree, and it feels like my marriage is so far away from me. I start helping Sam glue photos to the poster board.

"I don't just hate my life map," he says. "I hate all my classes."

Jimmy mops the bacon with a paper towel and acts like he doesn't hear even half of what gets said in his house.

He nudges Sam with his shoulder. "Want some? It's really good bacon."

Sam takes two pieces.

Then Charlie comes out of the little bathroom under the stairs. "What exactly are you doing now, Mom?" His bangs are sticking straight up in all the gel, which I guess is the look he wants.

"Helping Sam with his life map."

"Why isn't Sam helping Sam with his life map?"

"I like it. I like gluing photos on poster board."

Charlie takes a piece of bacon and leans against the orange counter and finishes in two bites. "Sam should glue his own photos. I had to do mine."

"Well, good for you, but I'm having fun."

"I can hear you." Sam stares at his brother. "I'm right here, Charlie. I can hear every word you say."

"Well, she's ruining your life by doing everything for you."

"You're ruining my life by being you."

Sam gets up and grabs his Shakespeare off the counter and goes and flops in Jimmy's recliner. "Why do people even *like* Shakespeare? It's not written in English."

"I never read a word of it." Jimmy takes more bacon.

"You don't have to *like* it," Charlie says. "Just *read* it and imagine you're in the story."

"Good idea, Charlie," I say. "Try what Charlie said."

"Who would ever want to be *in* a Shakespeare story?" He tosses the book on the floor. "Have you really read *Romeo and Juliet,* Charlie?"

"I've read the comedies and most of the tragedies."

"Because you wanted to?"

"I took the Shakespeare elective. Remember?"

"Fuck Shakespeare. It hurts my head."

"Sam," I say. "Stop it. I mean it."

"What? I *really* mean it. I don't understand the fake language. It seriously harms my brain."

"It's not fake," Charlie says. "It's the way people talked in the sixteen hundreds. It's about doing anything for love. It's the best play."

"You just like it because it's all about dying for a girl. No one should talk like that, ever." Sam stomps upstairs to put more clothes on.

"Yeah, *'dying for a girl,'*" Charlie calls up the stairs. "Get a vocabulary."

Jimmy starts laughing and goes and stretches out in the recliner and turns the NASCAR channel on.

I get up and look in the fridge. We're out of real milk, but I find a can of evaporated milk in the cupboard above the sink and make pancakes to help everyone feel better.

Charlie gets the first round and says they taste spongy.

"Thank you for that compliment," I say. "Give me strength."

Sam comes down the stairs in an old blue sweater of Kit's and a pair of sweatpants that balloon around his ankles and says, "You always say that, Mom. Strength for *what?*"

"Strength to get through another day with you."

Then I grab him and hug him before he turns away. It feels forced, but I do it anyway. Everything feels forced right now.

"Mom," he says after he eats his first pancake, "these taste sour. Like something sour is in them." He frowns.

I put the spatula down next to the frying pan and walk out the back door. I think I'll have a cry or some other form of big emotion out here, because the boys don't like my pancakes. I was trying hard with the pancakes.

It's freezing outside. The sky is a flat November gray, and Kit's gone. I came back to Maine for him, and he's left me here.

I turn and look at the house.

Charlie mashes his face against the window next to the door to try to get me to laugh. It doesn't work. But I go back inside without having any big emotion.

THE BOYS LEAVE AROUND five for a pep rally behind the high school. Sam's almost out the door when I catch him.

"Do you know how much I love you?"

"Mom." He scowls. "Don't ever say that."

"But do you know?"

"Mom, stop," he says. "You can't ever say that to me again."

The house is too quiet after they leave. Jimmy's out on the back stairs having his last cigarette. I'm going to make myself stay awake by working on the blue afghan I'm almost done with. I put on a rerun of *The Office.*

When Jimmy comes back in, I stand and try to give him the recliner, but he waves me off and says he doesn't own the chair.

Everything in the room looks preserved from when Martha lived here except for the recliner. There's the slatted-wood coffee table, and the mustard couch, and the matching turquoise lamps with horsehair shades.

Jimmy stares at the TV. Then he says he could never work in an office like that. He can only fish.

"Well, Kit may have to," I say. "Maybe he should take some of that money the state is giving to the fishermen whose quotas were cut so bad in the last round. Money for community college. Or computer training."

"Kit will no more work in an office than I will." Jimmy laughs. "Just shoot me."

I have all the pieces of the afghan done, and now I'm crocheting them together like my mother taught me. "He can't lobster. He can't shrimp. What is he supposed to do?"

"He's supposed to have his wife up at the hospital with him. We don't leave our sick, Jill."

"We do when we have teenage boys who need us."

"I see no one in need here. I see boys who could use a little toughening."

Now we are getting into it.

"You mean the way that you raised Kit? All that toughening? Because I don't think it worked, Jimmy. I don't think my boys need any more toughening. It's hard enough to be a boy these days."

"I raised Kit as best I could."

"You raised him?"

"I raised him. I raised Candy. I kept this roof over our heads. Candy has her stories. I know what she says. She's proud, like Martha was. You have no idea how Candy suffered after Martha died. No idea."

He stands and walks to the hallway. "But don't forget who their father was. You think a teenager knows how to raise a teenager?"

He goes upstairs, and my hands are shaking. I have to put the needles down.

CHARLIE COMES BACK HOURS later and says the pep rally was okay. Not great. Just okay. A few drunk idiots from the senior class brought fireworks and tried to ruin everything, but Principal Pierce was there. Charlie went to Lucy's afterward and lost Sam along the way.

"You were meant to stay together." I stare at him. I'm still getting over Jimmy's tongue-lashing. "What don't you understand about the word *together*?"

"I'm not his parent. That's what you keep saying. Besides, he's got his new friends."

"What friends?"

"The kid Roman and the other one, Derrick."

I give him a look.

"They're *fine,* Mom."

"Do any of them party?"

"Please don't use that word, *party.* You don't do it right."

"Okay. But do they?"

"I'd say it's *possible.*" He opens the fridge and pulls out the orange juice.

"Did you eat anything at Lucy's?"

"Lucy's mom made beef with vegetables and rice and spices. That's like the best thing I've ever eaten." He pours a glass of the orange juice and drinks the whole thing.

"Sounds so good. And you and Lucy?"

"What about us?" He places the empty glass in the sink.

"You're good?" I try to say this casually. I ought to be able to ask him.

He rolls his eyes.

"What's wrong with me asking? Tell me."

"The reason I like Lucy's mom is that *she doesn't ask me* stuff." He says this so sarcastically.

I'm kind of stunned. It's like he's fallen in love with the whole family. Lucy's mother and sister and three brothers. I want to show him that we can be a family too. Sam and Kit and Charlie and me. I just didn't expect to lose him so soon.

Candy told me that I have to be patient. There's no rushing it with teens.

I text Sam twelve times.

He doesn't text back.

Then he walks in around 1 a.m.

I stare at him and come out of the dream. "Where have you been?" It takes me another minute to get up from the recliner. "What have you been doing all this time?"

"We drove around."

He's over at the bottom of the stairs with his hands in the front pockets of his jeans.

"You drove where?"

"Just around."

"You drove around?"

"We ate at McDonald's. Went to Roman's to play songs. Why are you mad at me? Why are you like using that *tone*?"

"I'm not mad. I'm worried. And this is not a tone."

"No, you're mad and I did nothing wrong. I was just driving around. Jesus, Mom."

I can't believe he's acting like the person who's offended.

Kit used to spend all night driving with friends in cars. He said they'd drive and drive and end up at the McDonald's parking lot.

I go stand next to Sam at the bottom of the stairs and try to smell his breath and his hair. I can't find any evidence. But even I know there are ways to do drugs and not get caught.

"You broke curfew."

"What curfew?"

"The one where I said you needed to be home by eleven."

He shakes his head at me and walks upstairs.

I CAN'T SEE SAM'S face under the quilts. Only a swatch of his straw-colored hair. It's so dark outside it still feels like night. I put my hand on his back and press.

"Jesus, Mom." He rolls over. "What time is it?"

I whisper that he needs to go down to the store to stack boxes because he broke curfew.

He looks like he's going to fight me on this, but then he must decide he's going to lose anyway, so he grabs his sweatpants off the floor and follows me in the dark.

I turn the Mr. Coffee on, and he makes two pieces of toast and slathers them with honey.

"You must text me at night." I'm over by the back door in one of Kit's old flannel bathrobes, staring at the gravel driveway. "You must tell me where you are and what you're doing when your plans change."

"But the plans are always changing, Mom. That's the thing, okay? There are *no plans.*" He leans so far back in the kitchen chair that I think he's going to break the spindles.

"Promise me you'll text from now on. Promise."

He takes another big bite of toast. "Okay. Okay. I'm sorry. I'm really sorry. I don't mean to be such a jerk."

I point to the door. "Go help Candy."

WHEN HE'S GONE, I call Candy.

"It's still night out," she says. "Have you looked outside?"

"I know you're up."

She and Flip have been up since four. All the fishermen in Maine have been up since four.

"Well, I may be up, but I'm not human yet."

This means she hasn't had her first coffee.

"Take my younger son from me before I hurt him. Please."

"Send him down."

"I already have."

I GO BACK UPSTAIRS and pick Sam's jeans off the floor by the bathroom door. There's a little baggie of pot in the front pocket and the smallest clay pipe you can imagine. I walk downstairs and open the back door and stand under the pine trees and let myself get really cold to stop the zinging. It is so cold I could be at the South Pole. I'm no leader. I have not walked us to safety.

SAM COMES HOME MANY hours later and says it was really tiring at the store and that Candy was all worked up about how many boxes he stacked. He hopes I didn't tell her anything about the curfew, because she was acting odd.

"Please promise you didn't tell her anything, Mom?"

I almost start yelling at him then. But I'm still formulating my response to the pot.

He lies down on the couch and turns the TV on.

I stare at him from the hallway until I hope my eyes bore a hole in his head.

"Please don't do that." He takes a sip of water from the glass on the table. Then looks over at me.

"Do what?"

"Please don't stare at me like you've never seen me before."

. . .

I WAIT UNTIL DINNER. It's a long wait. Sometimes it takes just one moment to break through the normalcy of your life. Then so much else gets exposed. Your relationship to your children. Your borrowed house. The small film you're making and have secretly hoped will save your husband's village but will not really save anything. The anxiety grates on me. I call to the boys and put the baggie of pot on the table with the lasagna.

Jimmy's at the store, having a meeting with the lobstermen's association. I can do this my way. Except I don't really know what I'm doing.

"Oh good," Charlie says when he sits. "I was hoping to get high before we ate."

"Jillian," Sam says. "Jillian."

"Please don't call me that. Call me your mother."

My hands shake while I cut through the top layer of cheese on the lasagna and then down through the pasta and tomato sauce and beef.

"I can explain." Sam puts his face on the table next to his plate and closes his eyes.

"But will it do you any good?" Charlie asks.

Sam says he's sorry and that it is Robbie's pot. Sam's just taking care of it. "Keeping it so Robbie doesn't smoke it all."

If this is supposed to make me feel better, it's not. The pot looks old and brownish and is a symbol of how things are unraveling. There's a lot of pressure on the pot. The pot isn't just pot. The shirt in the bathroom in Nova Scotia isn't just a shirt.

"Oh really?" I say. "Like you're the foster parent for the pot?"

"Exactly."

"Sam."

He's not really here in the room with us. Maybe he's high. Does he think we're buying this?

"It makes me relaxed for like the only time in my life."

"Oh Sam."

"It's true, Mom."

"But you can't live this way, Sam." I look at his eyes.

First you have to get over the fact that they've even tried drugs. Then the fear becomes whether they'll like them when they try them. It's fear opening up upon fear.

He looks down at his plate.

"But I *can* live this way. I want to live this way. I like it."

"You used to be interested in fixing things with Dad and in making songs and in birds."

"I was six when I was interested in birds, Mom. It was like for a week." He makes a fist. "*Everyone* smokes pot. It's like a legalized substance, and you're completely out of control."

"But we're not everyone. And it's not legal. Unless you turned twenty-one and I missed your birthday. The pot's much stronger now, and you never know who'll get addicted." I thought he knew all this and that I saw too many addicted boys when I taught in the prison. The only thing I know how to do is to make it harder for Sam to do drugs.

"We do know, Mom. We do. You *can't* be addicted to pot, Mom."

"You can, Sam. Either way, what matters is not to do it. Give me your phone." I put my hand out. "Please just give it to me."

"I need it pretty much for my entire existence. I'll die without it. Please don't make me."

He's joking and not joking. He scares me a little.

This is when he should say sorry. He should say, Sorry for the pot, I'm really sorry, Mom.

He tosses the phone, and it lands in my lap. I feel a little victory about the phone, and then I crash.

I put it on the table next to my plate, but it's silly to take the phone. The flimsiest consequence. What will I do with the phone, anyway? I need him to have it, especially now, so I can keep track of him.

People told me you can run out of options when you have teen wolves. I didn't believe them. The mothers at the library story hours and the back-to-school nights. I thought I understood Sam, and this was all that mattered. I thought I'd never need to take his phone away, and I'd never run out of options.

I think the boys are waiting for what I'll say next. I am waiting too. Kit should be here. It would be better if he was here and we were together.

Charlie finally gets up and puts our plates in the dishwasher.

"I don't need to go to school," Sam says. "I want to be a fisherman."

"You can be. Just one who graduates from high school. But I thought you wanted to play in your band when you graduate."

Charlie says, "I think bands are an excuse to do drugs."

"Shut up, Charlie. You don't know fuck about bands."

"Sam!" It's the first time I've let myself yell in days. "You can't lie to me! You can't lie! Honesty is everything. Where do you get the pot?"

"Mom," he says. "Sometimes you can't take the truth."

Charlie's hanging by his fingers from the little molding above the kitchen door. I look over at him, and he shrugs. "It's true, Mom. Sometimes it's better to give you the facts in pieces."

"I'm not going to change who I am," Sam says, and goes and lies down on the couch.

Charlie follows him in there and stretches out in the recliner. "I can't believe what comes out of your mouth, Sam."

I leave the phone on the table. Sam can have his phone. What good does his phone do me?

I go sit on the arm of the couch. "Sam, if you're not going to stop smoking pot, then you're not going to live with me and Charlie and Jimmy." It's too hard to try to find the right words. "I'm not asking you to change who you are. I'm asking you not to do drugs, which doesn't seem like much."

Is anything getting through?

"Jesus." Charlie shakes his head.

"Jesus me? Or Jesus Sam?" I can't tell who Charlie's mad at.

"Just Jesus," he says, and turns on the TV.

I stare at the basketball game and miss the island and miss my bedroom with the peeling windowsills. We can never live in Jimmy's house again. Something in this house brings out the worst in us.

Charlie goes upstairs and comes down carrying three notebooks and says that he's driving to Lucy's to study.

I won't let him go. The roads have black ice.

He says he and Lucy have a *plan* and that they only have this one last year together in high school before she leaves for college. He has to go to her house.

I hate it when Charlie's mad at me even more than I hate it when Sam's mad at me. But the roads are really bad.

Then he mopes around the kitchen, opening and shutting the plywood cupboards, looking for things to eat.

"Did you *not* get more salt-and-vinegar potato chips like I asked?"

"Wait," Sam says from the couch. "You're not actually crying over potato chips, are you, Charlie?"

JIMMY'S STANDING IN THE hall outside my bedroom an hour later.

"Jill," he says, "you need to know that Sam's downstairs having
a shit fit in the kitchen about you taking his phone."

I climb out of the waterbed. It takes a minute. When I open
the door, Jimmy looks older than he did a few hours ago. Craggy
nose and white beard. Why haven't I noticed that he's lost almost
all his hair?

He's lived in Sewall all his life. This staggers me. Don't let that
become my husband. Don't let that become Kit.

He says, "Why in God's name doesn't someone bring these
boys up right?"

"Sam can have his phone, Jimmy. The phone is the least of our
problems."

"It's none of my business, Jill. Your marriage. But if you aren't
driving up to that hospital to get him, then I am. People go to hos-
pitals to die. Martha would want him home, and I'll be damned
if we're going to lose his boat. But I will tell you right now that
someone needs to give that Sam a talking-to."

I can see down to the front yard through the round window
at the end of the hallway. The grass is brown and frozen over
with ice.

As if I'm not trying to talk to Sam. As if it isn't all I think
about.

Jimmy's face is red and swollen with emotion. I've never seen it like this. He says, "Someone needs to get that boy on the water and out of his own head. He reminds me of the way I was, hell on wheels. Get him down to Shorty's tomorrow. Shorty says he's waiting for him."

"He has school tomorrow. He's sixteen, Jimmy. It's important he go to school. Shorty would be better off driving you up to the hospital to get my husband discharged. Please tell Kit I say hello while you're there. Tell the cook on the boat hello too. As for talking to my son, Jimmy, yeah. I've been trying to talk to him all along."

Then I close the door gently in Jimmy's face.

CHARLIE GOES UP TO Bangor with his debate team after school on Monday. The freezing rain starts at about five o'clock, and the roads get even icier. He calls from the bus on the way home. Is it okay if he sleeps at Lucy's house? She's *fine* with it.

It means I won't have to drive up in the dark and grab him at school.

I say yes, because the Subaru tires are old and don't do well on ice.

I don't know if I should talk to Lucy's mother about this. Maybe she thinks I'm crazy, letting my son sleep at her house.

Charlie says he'll sleep in the storage room in their attic.

Sam gets a ride down the peninsula with Robbie's mother. I know she drives a Range Rover because Sam has told me about this car many times. Its heated seats and sunroof.

I meet them outside their gate, and Sam climbs into the Subaru. It's raining too hard for me to get out and thank Robbie's mother. I think her name is Gwen. All I can do is wave through the fogged windshield and hope she sees me.

Sam and Jimmy and I watch *Jeopardy* that night, and Sam pouts on the couch because I didn't let him stay at Robbie's and play video games. But I was never going to let him stay. It's a school night. I'm trying to hold on to some of the routines at Jimmy's. It's been three months since Kit left. It feels like three years.

Tonight it's a full moon high tide, and Jimmy walks down to the harbor to see how far the water has risen. He comes back and says the waves are breaking three feet from Candy's house on the ledge. It's the highest waterline he's ever seen. He sits down in his recliner and shakes his head.

WHEN CHARLIE GETS HOME Tuesday night, Sam's making grilled cheese. The Celtics have won, and Jimmy's gone to bed. Charlie hangs his parka on the doorknob in the back hall and comes into the kitchen and opens the fridge.

I've missed him. It's surprised me how much. He was gone one night, and it felt like a week. When he's really gone and no longer lives with me, I'll need grief counseling. I'm only partly joking.

Sam says, "We've decided there's another word for it, Charlie."

"Word for what?" Charlie says.

"For sleeping over," Sam says. "We call them soirées." He flips one of the grilled cheeses with the spatula.

"We do?" I take a sip of my mint tea at the table, where I'm trying to edit Shorty's interview. "I have no idea what Sam's talking about, Charlie."

"I don't sleep in Lucy's room, if that's what you're thinking, Sam. I sleep in a room upstairs like an attic with all these boxes." He gets out the orange juice and pours a glass.

"What we want to know"—Sam turns the front burner off and puts the sandwiches on the cutting board and slices them in half so the cheese oozes—"is if you used protection."

Then Charlie pulls Sam down, and they go at it on the linoleum.

Every few seconds I tell them to stop. But I have no control over it, really.

When Charlie feels he's won, or has caused enough pain to scare Sam, he climbs off.

What amazes me is that Sam still doesn't let up.

"Well, did you do it?" he asks, and bites into his sandwich.

"Do what?"

"You know. Go all the way."

"Sam," Charlie says. "Get a life."

"I'm trying. But my mother won't let me out of the house. I'm being kept hostage."

"Not true." I go stare out the living room window. "Not true. Not true." I'm guilty of things, but that isn't one of them.

The waves in the harbor have little pointed tents on top that rise and fall, over and over. I think Lucy has saved Charlie by giving him a place for his emotions. But Sam doesn't have any place for his emotions to go.

Kit calls, and I answer on the first ring.

The bifocal doctor says he'd like to speak to me. Before I can say anything, he gets on the phone and tells me that the blood infection is a little better but they still don't know when Kit will be released.

"I don't like infections," the doctor says. "They make me angry."

"Okay." I try to make my voice upbeat. "This sounds good."

The boys are on the couch now, eating Breyers mint chip out of the carton with spoons.

The doctor says, "Just to be clear, it is not good."

"Great," I say. "Thank you so much." I take some small pleasure in hanging up on him.

"Dad's bad," Sam says, and stretches his arms up toward the ceiling.

"What are you talking about?" I walk into the kitchen. "The doctor said things were steady."

"But not really, Mom." Sam follows me. "I could tell by your tone. I can always tell by your tone."

Jimmy comes down to the kitchen and looks hard at Sam. "Be nice to your mother."

I can't believe he's on my side now.

"Mom lies, Charlie," Sam says. "She's not honest."

"I do not lie."

"Do too."

"You both have to go upstairs," I tell them. "I can't take you another minute."

"There," Sam says. "See? She's trying not to talk to us. That's how she lies."

I take Sam's shoulders and walk him to the bottom of the stairs. "How much are you brushing your teeth?"

"I've never even had a cavity."

"But you're older now. Brush twice a day. We can't afford cavities."

"We can't afford anything. What did the doctor really say, Mom?"

I steer him up the stairs into the bathroom and hand him his toothbrush from a blue cup Jimmy keeps on the sink.

I say, "It's the infection again."

He stops brushing and leans his face close to my face. "What are you even *saying*?"

"But we're still shooting for Saturday."

"If he doesn't make it back Saturday, my trust in you is completely lost."

I want to tell him that we're all suffering. And that it's time for him to grow up and stop taking jabs at me. Because he wears me down and this is how he wins.

"It's so lame of the doctor. So beat. This whole town is beat.

This whole state, and we should be there with Dad. We should totally be there."

"What about school?"

"What about it? All my grades suck."

"I know that isn't true. I think you have too much homework and that we need to get you out of some of those classes."

"It makes me want to scream when you say that. I want to take my punishment like everyone else."

"But school's not meant to be punishment, Sam."

"Do not even start with that stuff. This is serious."

I try to hug him by the sink, but he turns away.

"Mom." His face gets red. "His boat almost blew up. What does school matter? Stupid, stupid school." Then he walks out of the bathroom.

JIMMY AND CANDY LEAVE for Nova Scotia Friday morning before the sun's up.

I go out to the driveway to thank them. Candy's behind the wheel, and she rolls down her window and tells me to go back inside.

I say I'm embarrassed I'm not the one going, and that I'll have a bed set up in the living room for Kit by the time they get back tomorrow.

The sky is gunmetal gray, and it's starting to sleet. A loneliness creeps into everything I say. "Be careful," I warn her. "Drive slow. You don't have to go. I can go. I can do it."

She says he's her brother, *for God's sake.* "Of course we're going. Now get back inside, Jill, and dry off. We're a family. *Always have been, always will be.*"

I'M AT THE KITCHEN table that afternoon editing on my laptop when Sam walks in and says he's been kicked off the basketball team.

At first I don't understand what he's telling me.

Then he says he wants to jump off a bridge.

"That's not even funny." My eyes sting from the computer screen.

"It's true, though."

"What did you do?" I stand up from the table. "Tell me what you did this time."

He pulls up the hood of his sweatshirt and ties it under his chin. Then he shakes his head at me and goes and lies down on the couch. "It's bad. It's bad this time. You don't want to know."

"You didn't really get kicked off, did you?" I follow him. "Tell me you didn't."

"No, I did."


CHARLIE COMES HOME MAYBE ten minutes later and stands in the hallway and tells me that lots of kids smoke pot in the school parking lot, over by the big piles of sand. But it's pretty hard to get caught. Teachers don't go out there to check very often. But Sam's managed to do it.

Principal Pierce calls an hour later and says that in addition to being removed from the basketball team, Sam's been suspended from school for three days.

What will he do with his time? This is what I want to ask them all. What do you think he'll do with his time?

If boys don't fill it with basketball and debate team and science experiments, they find other things to fill it with, and this is how they start to get lost. When a boy gets kicked off the basketball team, it's everything.

AT SOME POINT NEAR dark, I make the boys bring down one of Kit's old twin beds so he can sleep in the living room. There will be no stairs for him for weeks. The bed is heavy and it takes some yelling and maneuvering to get it down. First Charlie yells at Sam about not listening to his directions, and then Sam yells at Charlie for bossing him.

We decide to put the bed by the far wall next to the couch, coming out vertically so Kit can lie in the bed and see through the hallway to the kitchen.

When we've got the bed where we want it, Sam tells me that he and Roman and Robbie may take their band to Burlington before school's even over.

"How will you do that?" I'm sitting on the arm of the couch, trying to have a concerned look on my face.

"Roman's van."

"But what about school? And will you get a job to pay for the trip?"

"I'll get a job, but not Roman. He says he has a learning disability. I'll do some independent study or something to get my credits."

I look out the window. Three cormorants are standing way down on Shorty's pier with their heads tucked under their wings.

Where's Sam getting the pot? How much is he smoking?

"A learning disability that prevents him from working?" Charlie yells from the kitchen where he's making tuna supreme.

"He gets money from the government. Or his parents do. And he volunteers."

"Who does?" Charlie says.

"Roman. Because he can't get a real job and make more than the minimum wage or he'd lose the government money. But it's not enough."

"What is not enough?" I don't understand.

"The *government money,*" Sam says.

"How do you *know* this?" Charlie says. "How do you know all these really personal things about him?"

"It's our band, Charlie. It's our *band,* all right?"


A STORM COMES THROUGH later, and the hard rain pelts the shingles on Jimmy's roof.

Charlie's over on the couch with his biology book. He says it's Sam's turn to bail *The Duchess.*

Sam's down on the floor, leaning against the couch, tossing a basketball over his head and watching the Celtics.

He says, "It's not like I'm *addicted,* if that's what you think, guys."

"Addicted to what?" Charlie asks.

"It was an experiment."

"What was?" Charlie says.

"Smoking."

"That's what you said the last time." I'm sitting in the recliner trying to enjoy the sound of the rain.

"I wanted to see what it was like," Sam says.

Part of me wants to get up and shake him.

"I'm only doing what every teenager in America does."

"Shut up, Sam," Charlie says.

"But I don't have a problem.*"*

"You smoked pot in the school parking lot when you were under contract with the basketball team." It's important to state the facts.

Charlie puts his book down and looks at his brother. "Where did you get the weed?"

"I should leave," Sam says. "I should just leave this state."

"*The Duchess* is sinking, Sam," Charlie says. "You need to go bail it."

Sam throws the ball up and catches it. Throws it again. This time it hits the water glass on the coffee table, and water spills over Charlie's math notebook.

Charlie leaps off the couch and tackles Sam down to the floor.

"Are you gonna bail the boat?" Charlie says. "Say it. Say you will." Charlie has an edge to his voice that I haven't heard before.

"Fine," Sam says. "I'll bail the goddamn boat."

He goes in the back hall and puts Kit's rubber boots on.

"This family is killing me."

When he's like this, we have to leave him until he figures out a way to forgive us for the things he's holding against us that we haven't done.

"I'm leaving." He has his hand on the doorknob. "This is me. I'm really going now."

AN HOUR GOES BY. Then another. I make an apple crisp and try to pretend Sam's not out in the freezing rain without a coat.

He doesn't come home for the Cleveland Cavaliers versus the Oklahoma Thunder on ESPN. I stand next to the recliner, listening to the rain and looking out the window waiting to see his shape walk up the dark hill.

I call Kit at eleven.

He answers and says, "Jimmy brought chewing tobacco and Candy's making me shave my beard. I think I'm going to get out of here."

"Well, we could use you here. Sam's out in the rain without a coat. It's been three hours, and it's almost snowing, and he's no longer on the basketball team."

"What do you mean, no longer on the team?"

"Meaning he got kicked off for smoking pot, and we had a deal."

"Who did?"

"Sam and me."

"What deal, Jilly? Can you just slow down a little, babe?"

"He promised. At least I think he promised."

"He promised what?"

"He promised not to smoke pot, and you ruined everything."

"Please don't call to insult me. Please don't. Please slow down. Teenagers do things, Jilly. They do things."

"I don't think they have to do things. Charlie doesn't do things."

"You don't know that."

"I've been devoted to them."

"You don't own devotion." His voice rises. "Jilly, where's Sam? I want you to slow down and tell me where you think he is."

"I bet he's down with Flip watching TV. Or over at Shorty's. Or Robbie's. Or in Avery with Roman or Derrick from the basketball team. He doesn't have a coat," I remind him. "No coat."

"Why no coat?"

"I think it was an act of protest."

Kit says, "Should we call Tim?"

Tim's been the sheriff in Sewall for the last ten years. He was one grade ahead of Kit in high school.

He says, "I'll call Tim and Flip and Shorty. You should sleep."

"You know I can't."

I hang up and get in the Subaru and drive around the village twice. Then I park outside the store and reach Candy at the hospital.

She's calling everyone she knows now up and down the coast.

It's midnight, and I leave two messages at Robbie's house, but I don't have a number for Roman's or Derrick's. I drive back to the A-frame and lie on the couch with my phone, waiting for Sam to call.


CHARLIE FINDS ME HERE on the couch at six o'clock in the morning and is really disturbed by this.

"We sleep in beds, Mom. That is why we *have* beds."

"Sam didn't come home last night."

"I know this. I share a room with him, remember?"

He seems calmer than I am. He almost always is. He says he thinks Sam's gone back to the island and we need to go out there and look.

I'll do anything anyone suggests. I put the amoeba coat on and the puffy gloves and follow Charlie down to the wharf. Steam curls off the harbor, and there are lots of seagulls standing on the ledge, waiting out the wind.

I take one glove off and call Lara. She doesn't answer.

*The Duchess* is still tied up to Jimmy's wharf. Charlie says it would be just like Sam to hitch a boat ride to the island and that we still have to go look.

It takes us ten minutes. We have to keep our chins tucked into our coats to stop them from freezing. Charlie docks the boat and jumps out and ties the stern line to the float. I do the bow.

The rooms inside the house seem smaller and colder now, and two ghosts live here. I've got to get outside.

We take the path through the woods to the southern tip. The ocean today is a cold, possessing ocean. The sound of the waves crashing against the rocks is a religious sound. Like the sound of the organ at the church my mother used to take us to.

I talked on the phone with her yesterday before Sam had gone missing. She said she needed more oxygen now and that my father was off getting several of her tanks filled.

She has long believed that Sam became a changed person when Liam fell off the bridge and that Sam saw the truth up there. This is what she calls it.

It's too cruel to make her worry about him now.

I stomp my feet. "I'm cold. Are you?"

Charlie's next to me, staring out to sea. "I was waiting for you to say something."

"Let's go back then."

He turns toward the path, and I follow him through the woods.

HE DOCKS THE BOAT at Jimmy's wharf, and we climb the hill and get in the Subaru and drive to Liam's family's farm. I'm grateful Charlie doesn't question me on this. I don't know why I didn't think of the farm before.

Liam's father, Jorge, comes out of the barn when I pull in. He's thinner since Liam died, and his face is much more lined. It holds more of the pain than Sally's face does, so in this way Jorge's face is proof, and you don't have to guess at his pain or try to read Jorge's mind. Sally met him on a painting fellowship in Ecuador. He's an expert in the science of organic vegetables. She's told me before she wishes she could look sad like him so people wouldn't expect her to be as sunny as they do. She says people still tell her how sorry they are for her loss. Then she has to smile at them with her apple cheeks and appear much happier than she really is.

After Liam died, Sam kept going to the farm. He told me that he *knew* Liam wouldn't be there but he thought maybe there was a chance something else would happen. Some message or something, he said. Some feeling. He was only fourteen.

In those years Jorge and Sally were his second parents. We called each other that. Jokingly. We had no idea what we were saying.

Charlie follows Jorge into the barn, and Sally comes outside and lets out a little yell when she sees me. Her dark curls bounce when she does her little jump. Then she claps her hands, and leads me into the kitchen. It was her grandparents' kitchen, then her parents', and now hers. The whole house is low and narrow, with old pine floors and no dishwasher or shower, so they've only ever taken baths.

"When did you last see him?" She puts the red kettle on.

"When he went out to bail the boat last night."

Molly, their youngest, is in the den off the kitchen at the table they use for jigsaw puzzles. Sally nods her head toward her and says they're homeschooling her now because she's having a hard time with friends. Their other daughter, Leela, is consumed by ice hockey.

"The girls miss Liam in different ways," Sally says. "One uses it as a strength, and the other can't get over it."

I think Sam uses it as a strength too, but it's also something he can't get over. He doesn't talk about Liam, ever. It hits me that I haven't asked him for a long time how much he misses Liam. It's something you would think I'd have asked. The most obvious thing, really, but I believed I was protecting Sam by not asking. When really all I've probably done is make Sam feel more alone.

He's not here. That's been clear since we got out of the car.

What am I doing here? It feels wrong to have brought my worry.

I remember the night they found Liam's body. How afterward, when the identification was over and there was nothing left to do, Kit drove the four of us back to Liam's house and we stood in this kitchen. There was nowhere to go look for Liam anymore. Time stretched out ahead for so long that it looked cruel.

I take the tea from Sally, but I can't drink it. "I think I've got to go find Sam."

"Of course you do." She waves her hands at me. "Go. Go."

I wish I'd called her first and hadn't driven my worry over and put it at her feet. I wasn't thinking.

Outside, Charlie and Jorge are leaning against the green trac-
tor. Jorge says it was good timing that we came when we did,
because he needed help with one of the wheels.

Charlie looks pleased to be of service.

But when we get in the car, he's furious. He says it's all for
attention, the way Sam's gone missing.

"It doesn't matter what it is," I tell him. "Because we have to
find him."

I back the car up to the road and pull out. I'm thinking about
how Sally is able to go on without Liam. I said something about
this to her right after he died. I was cooking her pasta while she
sat on their blue sofa next to the woodstove. I kept wanting her to
rest, and she kept saying she was better off moving. But she hadn't
slept in so many hours.

I told her that I couldn't imagine how she was feeling.

She said I *could* imagine it. "Just by asking me about it, you've
imagined it, Jill."

I couldn't tell if she was angry at me or sad. Or both.

"I think every mother has imagined it in some way." Then she
stretched her legs so that her bare feet almost touched the front of
the woodstove, and it looked like she was going to burn herself.
"But it's not like that. You wake up each day. You don't choose. It's
not that easy. I wish it was. If it happened to you, Jill, if you lost
Sam, you'd live for Charlie, just like I'm going to live for my girls.
If I can do it, you can."

WE GET TO ROBBIE'S gate, and I say, "Hello? Hello!" into the black speaker nailed to a wooden post by the gate. I push the button again. "Hello? Is anybody in there?"

Charlie closes his eyes, willing this to be over.

"It's Jill Archer! Looking for Sam. Has anyone in there seen him?" I keep my voice high so it's easier to understand me.

Robbie's mother's voice is garbled when she comes on, so it's like she's talking underwater. She was a real estate agent in Virginia, and I've only met her twice since they moved here three years ago. She says she hasn't seen Sammy. But she likes him very much. "What a good boy he is!"

Then she wishes us luck. She'll let me know if she hears absolutely anything.

There's a big piece of granite next to the gate that has the family name carved on it. FELDER. I turn the car around slowly, making sure not to hit it.

When we're back on the main road, Charlie says, "Why does she talk in that accent?"

"Because she's from Virginia."

"But why would you ever leave Virginia? It's *warm* in Virginia."

It's the time of the year here when winter looks hard and long and we fixate on warmer places and end up talking about these places as if they're options. When they're not really, because we'll never actually go anywhere.

"Why does she call him *Sammy?*" Charlie presses his hand against his window and traces it with his finger. "Who is Sammy?"

I'VE BEEN TO DERRICK'S only once before, to pick Sam up after a basketball team dinner. He lives in an old Cape, about two blocks from the YMCA. I leave Charlie in the car, and when I get out, the German shepherd tied to the tree next to the house goes a little crazy.

The front door is a dark blue and has a gold knocker hanging on it. I try lifting the knocker up and letting it fall several times, but no one comes. Then I bang on the door with my hand.

The dog barks, and I keep knocking. I think Sam's hiding in there, and it's a terrible, humiliating feeling. He's not coming to the door because he knows it's me.

I turn and wave at the dog and tell it I come in peace. "Please. Please stop barking at me."

The dog doesn't stop, and Sam doesn't open the door.

I get in the car and close my eyes and Charlie tells me to just try to breathe.


CANDY CALLS WHEN WE'RE about halfway down the peninsula. She says Flip has everyone on the lookout. "Every fisherman on this part of the coast, Jill."

"That's good. That's really good."

"Would you like to speak to your husband now?"

I shake my head no. "Just tell him to call me if he hears anything."

I have an urge to go as far away from Sewall as possible, so Kit will have to look for me, and I'll be looking for no one. When he finds me, he will say how sorry he is and that he can't live without me even for a day.

Then I park outside the A-frame and lose the thread of my marriage and all the emotion I just had around it. Charlie and I walk inside and begin waiting again.

THERE'S A NEW POST on Sam's Instagram around noon. A boy I don't recognize, from a different high school, who's standing on a stone wall in what looks like a cemetery, wearing his baseball hat backward. *#brosforlife #basketballislife*

WHEN I CAN'T TAKE the A-frame any longer, I leave Charlie there and go back to Avery and drive around town in circles.

Lara calls and says she's coming up.

"Please don't." Part of me thinks Sam's in Portland by now, and that Lara will get a call soon asking her to pick him up. Sam will sound sheepish on the phone and explain it was all a stupid joke.

"This is going to be okay," Lara says. "Listen. I bet he's at Robbie's house now eating nacho Doritos."

"How do you know that?

"Please do not think the worst."

"What if he's trying to hitchhike to Nova Scotia?"

"He's not," she says. "But I'm right here standing by."

I do loops for another hour past the high school and the Shell station and the credit union and Anthony's with the sign in the shape of a pizza.

I'm about to give up when I see Sam coming out of the 7-Eleven across Middle Street.

No coat, just LeBron James over some long-sleeved black T-shirt. How I know he's drunk is that he keeps putting his hands on Derrick's shoulders and jumping up on Derrick's back and screaming his name.

It's horrible to watch. I don't know him, and I know him so well.

Derrick does not appear drunk. He's got a six-pack of Coke under his right arm, and he walks in a straight line to his truck.

Sam stops to bang on the hoods of many of the cars in the parking lot.

If Kit were here with me, he'd get out now and confront Sam and put him in the Subaru and drive him home. But I don't see how that will work, or how I can convince Sam. I think the whole point for him will be not to get in the car with me and to make a show of it.

I watch him bang on more cars, and I think I might die while I watch or melt into the floor of the Subaru or something. There's so much emotion in him. Who is he? How little I know my children. How little I know Sam. How much he keeps from me.

I call Lara. "I almost have him."

"What do you mean 'almost'?"

She wants me to get out of the car and confront him. "Just try it."

"No way. You don't get it. You can't see how scary he is. You would not believe it."

She stays on the line while Derrick opens the truck's driver's-side door and climbs in the truck. Then Sam opens the passenger door and hoists himself up beside Derrick. They look like grown men in there, because of the way the truck seat makes them appear much taller than they are. But they are boys and one of them is drunk.

"What am I supposed to do now?" I ask Lara.

"You're supposed to follow that truck. Do not let the truck out of your sight."

THE TRUCK TAKES ME back to Derrick's. I pull over on the road, across from the driveway, and call Kit. How can he not answer?

I wait for the beep. "I've got him," I say. "I found him."

I can't remember if Kit even understands how to check messages.

Then I call Charlie and tell him that his brother is at Derrick's and appears to be drunk.

"Oh, thank God." He says it again. "Thank God." Then there's a pause. "Figures he would be *drunk*. What an idiot. Who *does* that? Who doesn't call us for a day and goes and gets drunk?"

I tell him to let it go. "Go to Lucy's like you planned. Sam is fine," I say. "Your brother is good."

I drive down the driveway and park in the dirt by the truck. I have all the adrenaline again.

When I get out, the German shepherd starts barking and pulls so hard on its chain I'm afraid the dog will choke.

Derrick's mother opens the door and smiles at me. "Leslie?"

She nods her head and says she's terrible with names.

I say, "Jill," and she says she knew it was something like that and we both laugh.

She's got on blue scrubs like she did at the school gym.

"I'm sorry Steve has such bad manners."

I realize she means the dog.

She looks over at him. "Steve, give us a break now, okay? Stand down, Steve. Stand down."

The dog stops barking and stares off in the distance.

"Come in. Come in, come in." She closes the door behind us and says the boys are sleeping but she can go wake them. "They're good boys. Such good boys."

I don't ask why she thinks the boys are sleeping at five o'clock on Saturday. Or why she doesn't have any of my skepticism. I don't see how the boys could be asleep. They just got here.

I'm thinking about how to get Sam in the car without a scene. Lara and I decided back at the 7-Eleven that it will be better for me to have witnesses when I try to make him come home with me. Actual people watching. Then maybe he won't fight me.

There are three more dogs behind a wooden baby gate in the kitchen. Each some kind of shepherd mix, I think. I don't see Sam.

Leslie calls for the dogs to stop barking. "More bad manners." She laughs. "You can probably tell I have a problem saying no to rescue dogs."

I smile at her.

Please go wake my son up.

"Let's go see what those turkeys are up to." She climbs over the gate, and her long hair swings from side to side. The dogs disappear down the hall behind her.

I tell myself not to be angry when I see him. I want to be open and calm, so we don't start fighting again.

But when he comes into the kitchen and climbs over the gate, I'm furious. It's a wave of emotion that I can't control. A long-fomented rage.

Why didn't he call me? Why didn't he have the decency to call? I'd begun to think the worst things.

"You're here." I try to make my voice sounds neutral. I can't smile at him. That's asking too much. "You're really here."

"Yeah, I'm here, Mom. This is me." He leans against the wall next to the baby gate and closes his eyes for a second.

I raise my eyebrows at Leslie. Then I turn and walk toward the door, hoping Sam will just follow me out of habit or something.

Please don't make a scene.

I get to the door, and he's right behind me, so I stop and hold it open for him and wait for him to pass. Then I wave at Leslie and mouth the words *thank you*. I have no idea if she understands that my son's drunk.

When we're out in the yard, I want to yell, and it takes restraint not to. I say, "It's hard to understand what's happening here. Very hard."

He says nothing.

We get in the car, and he leans against the window and closes his eyes.

I say that he smells like a fermentory.

"What the hell does that mean?"

"The place where they make the alcohol." But sarcasm doesn't help, and I would like to stop using it.

What I really want to say is how scared I've been, and what is bothering you so much that you would run away?

WBLM plays two Tom Petty songs in a row, which makes me think of Liam. Liam's gone, and Sam is banging on the hoods of cars in parking lots.

I look at my phone at the stoplight. Six messages from Kit. Two from Candy. We pass the Trading Post with the AMMO 4 SALE sign. After all this time, I don't know what's required of me to meet Sam where he is. The most devout people at my mother's church talk about surrendering. I'm willing to try to surrender, if it would help Sam. But it feels like I surrendered a while ago.

"I'm sorry," he says then. "I'm sorry, I'm sorry, I'm sorry."
Sorry counts. Sorry is something.

I drive past Andy's Gun Shop and the grange hall. The view
to the ocean is unobstructed now, and there's an important meeting of terns down at the waterline.

I don't think the say-very-little strategy is working, so I aban-
don it. "Why didn't you call me? I just don't understand why you'd
make us worry this way. It's cruel. You're cruel."

He says nothing to me.

HE TAKES HIS CLOTHES off in Jimmy's back hall. They're all damp. I give him Kit's old bathrobe, and he lies on the couch shivering and sort of wincing.

I don't say anything. I have no words really. I put one of the blankets over him and sit on the couch and take his feet in my lap and press on each of his toes.

I used to do this at night on the island when he was young. Press each toe before I left his room.

He closes his eyes. "Sorry. Sorry again for being such a fuckup."

"Shhhh." I keep pressing his toes.

I see you.

This is what me pressing the toes says. I see you and I'm not leaving. What I wish for him is some relief.

"You must have been cold outside without your coat on. I was worried about you. Very worried." I keep pressing his toes. I see you.

"I didn't feel cold at all." He still has his eyes closed. "I try not to feel anything. It's my new goal in life. To be numb."

I can feel his worries in the room with us. I hate that he has them and wants to be numb, when I'm right here with him. When I've been here the whole time. Right here pressing your toes, don't you see?

. . .

WHEN HE FALLS ASLEEP, I go into the kitchen to make him pasta with red sauce. I could be cooking anything. My brain isn't working. It's relying on some kind of muscle memory and calling up the past—three different boys from my high school in Harwich who are now dead. Two from drugs. One from a gun. And the boy, Michael, in the prison, who used to shoot slapstick comedies on my old video camera. How during class he'd put the camera down on the table that was bolted to the floor so he couldn't use it as a weapon, and he'd walk toward me.

I was meant to keep my finger on the button of the emergency beacon clipped to my jeans so if Michael came at me, I could press the button and two guards would come save me. But Michael would just ask if he could go to the bathroom, and then he'd say, help me. Please help me.

I know Sam will be hungry soon.

Candy calls and says they'll be here in thirty minutes.

"Who will?"

"Who do you mean *who*? My father and brother and me, for God's sake."

"You've got Kit?" I feel like Sam and I are alone in a dream and that we'll always be alone.

"I told you we wouldn't leave without him."

"Wow."

"Is that all you can say?"

"Yeah. Wow. You really have him?"

"God's truth. We're driving like banshees."

Oh Christ. I'm not ready for this.

PART SIX

**THEY ARE MY PEOPLE**

WHEN THE JEEP PULLS in, my thoughts go quiet. I walk outside and stand under the porch light and wait. Candy gets out of the car first and goes around to the side and opens the back door for him. I see the soles of his beat-up boots first, and then his legs.

He keeps the right leg extended while Jimmy goes behind the Jeep and gets the crutches out of the back and gives them to Kit. He takes one in each hand and lowers his legs down to the ground and moves his body to the edge of the seat so he's more out of the car than in it, then Candy and Jimmy help him stand.

Everything is in slow motion. I see how he can't go fast now, even if he wanted to. He makes his way toward me. Candy's got one hand on his back like she's helping him keep his balance, even though he's much taller than she is and double her body weight. He's got a small, nervous smile, and he shines it on me. I can count on one hand the times I've seen my husband nervous. His hair is short again and wavy and lovely. His face is pale and thin. God I know this face.

My heart does the leaping thing. I can't help it. He gets to the back door and has to take the three steps slowly, one by one, with the crutches. Then he's before me.

He bends down toward me, and I think he's trying to kiss me, but it's crowded with both of us on the landing, and I don't think he can reach my lips. I press my face against his chest. We don't kiss. I have these prepared speeches in my head about marriage and trust. But when I see him, I know I won't be giving any speeches tonight.

"It's me," he says.

"It's you."

"God, I missed you," he says, and his face is clear, like he's not hiding anything and is putting all his attention on me and is able to really be here.

Candy tells him to watch the last step up into the hall. It's higher than the last two. They walk by me, and I stand with my hand on the door, keeping it open for them. Kit places the crutches down on the hall floor and then uses his left foot, so the right foot just grazes the floor.

Jimmy is still out in the yard dragging some dead branches away from the driveway. I wait for him, then close the door behind him.

Kit's leaning on the crutches by the side of the couch when I get there. "Hello," he says to Sam. "Is anyone in there?" Then he bends down and puts his hand on the top of Sam's head.

It takes Sam a minute to process.

"You? Dad?"

"Yeah, me. What are you going to do about it?"

"You're *home?*" Sam looks maybe twelve years old. I bet the alcohol's wearing off. "You came *home?*"

"I was always coming home." Kit smiles.

Candy and I are both watching from the hall. She doesn't even try to stop her tears. I follow her into the kitchen, so no one sees mine.

"How in the world did you get him out of there?" I ask her.

She throws her head back and laughs. She's got on the long red cardigan from Walmart in Bangor that she loves. "I had Jimmy with me. He scared everyone in that hospital to death."

She gets a meat loaf that she probably made Jimmy weeks ago out of the freezer and puts it on a plate in the microwave. "Plus all his bloodwork was good. There was no way in hell those doctors were going to keep him any longer. Linda let everyone in the hospital know that Kit was going home to find his son."

"I honestly cannot believe you." I open the fridge to look for the Parmesan.

"You try spending that much time with my father in a car. What I need now is a cigarette."

Flip hates it when she smokes, and she hardly does it anymore. But I follow her outside and sit on the top stair while she lights up. She points at my T-shirt with her cigarette. "It's not summer, you know." She smiles. "It was much worse with Jimmy Junior. He took years."

Jimmy Junior is Shorty's youngest brother's son who has been in and out of rehab for what feels like the last decade.

"Therapy helped," Candy says. "And the legal drugs they used to wean him off the illegal ones."

I don't think Sam should be compared to Jimmy Junior. He doesn't have that kind of drug problem, but what do I know.

"I'm sorry you had to go get Kit. And I'm sorry about Sam. Sorry about all of this."

It's like she hasn't heard me. This is her way with certain emotions, especially apologies.

"Are you thinking you'll ever talk to your husband again? He's torn up. I've never seen him like this."

"I just didn't expect it, you know? He and I have been through stuff before, but I thought we were okay."

"Just talk to him, Jill." She puts the cigarette out under her boot. "The man is a mess."

"He hates talking, Candy. You know that."

"He'll have to talk. I make Flip talk. You can't get this far in a marriage without talking."

A car comes down the driveway in the dark and stops. Charlie gets out and waves at the driver. I walk toward the headlights.

"Go see what the cat dragged inside," Candy tells him.

He runs, and Candy and I follow him. Kit's lying on his back in the bed next to the couch, and Charlie's sitting on the floor by the bed, holding Kit's hand without any self-consciousness. Sam's propped his head up on one of the couch pillows, watching his brother and his father talk.

I shake my head and go into the kitchen and put the red sauce on the pasta. Candy slices the meat loaf and calls for everyone to come get a plate.

Jimmy takes his food to the recliner and turns the college football on. He says the Patriots will need better offensive linemen for the game tomorrow.

Candy brings Kit some meat loaf and a little spaghetti. He leans his head against the wall and eats in the bed and says they'll need more than offensive linemen.

I'd forgotten how he and his father finish each other's sentences.

Sam walks into the kitchen in the old bathrobe and makes a plate of food. No one says anything about the bathrobe or the fact that he's up and moving. He brings his dinner back to the couch and sits down next to Charlie. There's a shell-shocked ordinariness about us.

When we finish eating, Candy announces that we're all going to bed.

It's only nine-thirty, but even Charlie, our biggest night owl, agrees.

Jimmy says he's moving to Candy's, and goes upstairs to get clothes. Candy walks over to Kit's bed and asks if it's comfortable.

He says he's always wanted to try sleeping down here.

She makes a funny face at him and smiles and raises her eyebrows, like she's glad he's home but she's too emotional and if she says anything else to him she'll cry. She leans down and puts her arms around his shoulders. Then she's out the door.

Jimmy comes downstairs and goes over to the bed and says something to Kit that I can't hear. Then he puts a hand on Kit's shoulder and keeps it there for a second. I'm not sure I've ever seen them physical like this before.

After Jimmy leaves, the boys go high-five their father in the bed, and Charlie takes the crutches for a spin around the room. Then the boys fight a little about who will sleep on the couch next to Kit now that there's only one bed in their bedroom.

Charlie easily wins. Sam has no fight in him. He gives up quickly and walks upstairs. Charlie follows him up to the bathroom.

Kit puts his arm out like he's reaching for my hand.

I need something from him before I can take his hand. I don't know what it is. Some kind of penance or confession, no matter how bad it is.

"Come here, you." He smiles, but it's the nervous smile again. "Please come over here." He pats the quilt on the bed where he wants me to sit and give him some attention.

"I can't do this now," I tell him.

"Just sit with me. We drove all day so I could see you."

"I wish I could." I walk to the hall. "I hope you're warm enough in here. I hope you have enough blankets and that you sleep, and I'm glad you're home, Kit." Then I go upstairs.

I'M NOT EMBARRASSED TO say we make it through Sunday by watching a great deal of professional sports on TV. Nettie will see Sam at eight tomorrow morning. She's made a slot for him where there was no slot. When she called me earlier, she said she could hear the desperation in my voice on the message I left her late last night. I'm holding on to this appointment now. It feels like our best hope to try and understand what's happening to Sam. He's not talking to me really anymore. He keeps looking at me like who are you, living in this house with my father and me?

Lara calls in the afternoon, and I go upstairs to the bathroom, because it's the only place in the house where I think I can't be heard. I tell her the four of us ate pizza for lunch and watched the Celtics, and Sam was agitated during the game. Pacing and yelling at the screen. We could not get him to sit down. When the Celtics won, he jumped around and screamed and knocked over one of the ceramic lamps. Kit had to tell him to stop it.

"This is why I bow down to you. I could never handle parenting."

"No, you could."

"No. I couldn't. We both know that. So let me bow down. I've been thinking about Marsh. I've decided that she got cold on the boat and borrowed Kit's shirt and kept it afterward."

"I like your theory. But we both know it's not true. You should understand I've willed myself to never think about the shirt again."

"Very good. Keep doing that. And please will yourself to stay married."

"Like it's that easy."


NETTIE'S OFFICE WAS ONCE a Texaco station, and it still has the gray concrete floors and nubby white walls. Kit remembers getting gas here with Jimmy when he was really young. There's a blue-and-green swirled rug and a spider plant in a macramé holder. Sam and Kit are sitting on the maroon couch. Kit's crutches lean against the wall next to the couch. I'm over in an armchair that's also a rocking chair that rocks back and forth if I let it.

Nettie smiles at us and says, "It's nice to finally meet you, Mr. Archer."

Kit's never met her before and doesn't know what she requires, or that there's almost nothing she won't ask.

She's got on a dark paisley dress today, and her hair's pulled back in a braid. She looks like someone I'd want to tell my secrets to if I were Sam.

She says she's going to ask him the series of questions she asked him the first time she met him two years ago. She wants to see if any of his answers have changed.

She starts with hobbies.

He says his band and basketball. But he got kicked off the team and doesn't know if the coach will let him back on.

"School?" How does he like it?

He hates it. "Doesn't work for my brain."

She says, "It's good you're able to say how you feel" and writes something on her clipboard.

"But you're admired at school," I say.

He looks at me like I'm crazy.

"I don't know what you're talking about, Mom. I don't know anyone at school who admires me."

I clasp and unclasp my hands. It's warm in here, and I slide my feet out of the clogs and wish I could take back what I said.

"Mrs. Archer." Nettie smiles at me. "I like the way you show your support. But I want to hear from Sam right now. Let's have him drive the conversation today. In fact, what if Sam and I stay in here and you two go out to the waiting room? Can we do that? Sam and I will talk. Then we'll come find you."

It strikes me then how young she is. I don't think I hold this against her. I never thought I'd become an ageist. It's working for Sam. That's what I remember most from last time. How willing he is to talk to her.

THE WAITING ROOM HAS two black office chairs on wheels, and a black wooden bench, and an ugly glass coffee table. You can see all the electrical wiring in the ceiling and the heating ducts. I sit on the bench, and Kit just stands and leans on his crutches. He says it's too much work to try and sit down again and that Sam seems calmer today than he did yesterday. "He showed me his mustache this morning, or what he wants to be his mustache. He was the old Sam."

"He's been waiting for you. He's always better around you."

We've all been waiting. Resentment is a dangerous thing at a therapist's office, and I think Kit knows this too.

We stay in the waiting room for ten more minutes or so in a kind of duel where neither of us says anything.

Then Nettie invites us back in and says it's good we came to see her, because Sam is carrying things around with him that she'd like him to put down.

"We all know this," she says. "We all know Sam has strong

memories of Liam. What I don't think you're aware of are his over-riding feelings of responsibility for Liam's death. Am I getting this right, Sam?"

Sam nods at her and goes back to studying his high-tops.

"We've talked about it this morning," she says. "His survivor guilt. And how this guilt is still with him. I'm betting both of you are trying to help him put the guilt down. Would you say that, Jill?" She looks at me.

"Yes. I would say that."

"And you, Kit?" she says.

"Absolutely," he says.

"We all want to help take the guilt away and find a place for Sam to put it, but we don't know how." She leans forward so that she's at the edge of the wooden chair. "What I want you to see is that when Kit was in the accident in Canada, Sam began to do what we call spiraling. Another way we refer to this is doing stress. Sam's brain connected the accidents. Liam and Kit. And then he started doing a lot of stress. Sometimes his guilt is all he thinks about, which gets hard on his brain. So what we want him to know is that Kit's okay now. Kit isn't dying. Kit is right here."

Sam pulls on the neck of his sweatshirt.

I think I would have known if he was experiencing the kind of guilt Nettie's talking about. I think I would have been able to tell.

Nettie asks Sam to try to describe what it's like inside his brain.

I don't think he'll answer her.

He stares at his sneakers.

Just when I think he may never talk again, he says, "Liam like *takes over* everything."

"Everything?" I say. I can't help it. He can't mean *everything*.

"Yeah, everything," he says.

I get so sad for him then. Just so sad.

Nettie says, "I want you to know this is not a case of Sam keeping secrets, Jill. This is his brain needing help. Sam's brain needing a break."

I nod at her, and when I look over at Kit, he's nodding too.

Nettie says, "This is about you both seeing Sam."

But I see him.

"It's about not leaving him," she says.

I hardly ever leave him.

"Because Liam left," Nettie says.

"How this will look for Sam will be different on different days," she says, "but the important thing is that he keeps talking. Because to admit it really is half his battle. It really is."

She tells Sam that she's going to give him a scale for his brain.

"A what?" He looks up at her. "I don't need a stupid scale."

"It's easier not to love yourself, Sam. We just talked about this. It's always going to be easier to be negative than to love yourself."

He rolls his eyes at her.

I do not move in the rocking chair.

"So break that pattern right there," Nettie says. "Just break it. Don't go negative on us. That negativity you have is the most limiting emotion. I've never seen it do any good. I've only seen it ruin people. You hear me?"

He nods.

"And you see these people here?" She points to Kit and me. "You can just accept them. It would be easier. Accept them and the house you sleep in and the food they give you and their love. You can drop the mask and stop feeling like you're unseen."

He says, "But what does that even mean?"

"There it is again," she says. "Drop it. Don't try to blame me or them. We didn't make Liam fall off the bridge. You didn't make Liam fall either. He just fell. So let it go."

"Let what go?" He looks at her.

"Let the guilt go. The blame. Let it go. Let it go. You caused these two people in this room here so much worry when you ran away. Don't push yourself away from them."

She looks at me and smiles.

"And so this scale, Sam?"

He meets her eyes.

"This scale is so you can weigh the guilt you have and decide whether it's worth holding on to or not. Each time the guilt comes, you weigh it. Pretty soon I don't think it will follow you around so much. Then you won't feel the need to numb yourself. You just won't need to."

"That would be good." He looks so tired now. "Because I've got other things to worry about, like getting Coach to let me back on the team."

Nettie says that will all depend on his showing up every day at school. "That's all up to you. But this is where we start." She puts her hands on the tops of her thighs and stands. "We're helping you find places to put the guilt down and to stop doing stress. Does this sound like a plan, Sam?"

He doesn't look at any of us. But he nods at the floor.

IN THE CAR ON the way home he says, "Nettie told me my brain thought that Dad wasn't coming back."

"But I did come back." Kit turns in his seat, so he's facing him. "I told you I'd come back, and I did."

"I didn't really *think* Dad wouldn't come back. "Nettie says it's like my brain was tricking me."

"I was gone a long time," Kit says. "It was wicked scary."

"I mean, the boat was on fire," I say.

"But that hardly ever happens," Kit says. "Boats don't just catch fire. It won't happen again."

"Please don't say it won't ever happen again, Dad. Because it *could* happen. I mean, anything could happen. So you have to stop pretending and you have to stop assuming things about me."

"Assuming what things?" I ask.

"You always *assume* things, Mom. It makes me *crazy*. Like really crazy when you think I'm smoking weed all the time."

"I do not think that. Kit, have I ever said I think Sam's smoking weed all the time?"

"You have not."

Being a mother isn't anything like I thought it would be. It's harder. Better. More confusing. Shorter. Longer.

"See, Sam," I say.

"There you go again. Doing it."

"Doing what?"

*"Judging me."*

"I can't keep up with you. Tell me."

"Tell you what?" He closes his eyes.

Kit says, "Tell us how to be around you."

"Okay. Okay." He sits up. "Number one. Don't lie to me any-more. Only tell me the truth, like about Dad. Only the truth."

"I can do that," I say.

"Number two, don't make me go to school."

Kit says, "Let's just get through this week, Sam. Let's just see how this week goes. It could get better, you never know. Can we do that?"

I don't think he'll ever agree.

But then Sam looks at Kit, and we drive the rest of the way home in a truce.

LUCY COMES FOR DINNER that night. I try once in the middle of the afternoon to convince Charlie to change the plan, but he won't. He's fixated on it and says they've had it planned for weeks and how could I have forgotten?

She and Sam sit on the couch and try to answer the *Jeopardy* questions with Kit. She laughs whenever Sam gets an answer right, and somehow makes him talk. She's direct like this and treats him as an adult.

Charlie helps me with the chili. He seems really nervous, so I try to keep things loose. My head is full of different pieces of knowledge that it didn't have before we went to Nettie's this morning. The scale and Sam's guilt and where Sam's going to be able to put the guilt down, and will any of it work and will we know if it's working.

We bring our bowls of chili into the living room, and Charlie delivers one to Kit over on the bed, then he goes back and gets another for himself. He and Lucy sit on the couch together, while Sam sits in the recliner and stares at them.

I bring a chair in from the kitchen and put it over by Kit's bed, and he smiles at me and I can tell he likes that I'm there, closer to him. I can feel him wanting me to give him my attention.

Lucy says, "This is yummy, Mrs. Archer. This is delicious."

Sam tells her that Kit just got back from the hospital. "He was in Canada. A Canadian hospital."

"*Sam,*" Charlie says. "Of course she already knows that."

"My father is gone too." Lucy pulls the neck of her sweater over her chin. "At the camp in Kenya."

I knew about her father. I knew. But in an abstract way. Now I try to imagine it. The waiting for the visa. The separation. The feelings of such deep missing, and longing, and pain, and not knowing when it was going to end.

Her father told her that he was coming here right after her. But that was three years ago. Our government won't let him in, even though she says he may be killed if he returns to Burundi.

Jesus.

She gets up and goes into the bathroom under the stairs.

Should Charlie go check on her?

When Lucy sits back down, Charlie tells us that she applied early decision to Smith today.

Kit says, "That's fantastic news."

She shakes her head. "Charlie, come on."

Charlie says, "I bet they give her a full ride."

"There's no such thing as a full ride, Charlie." Lucy looks embarrassed but also proud. "There are just different ways of spelling the word *loan*."

I feel for a second like my work's done with Charlie. That Lucy's helped him become someone who talks about colleges and loans, and I'm sad about this. I don't know where the sadness comes from, but I don't want my work to be done with him. He's only seventeen.

When the boys bring the dishes back to the kitchen, I tell her to sit because she's the guest. But she won't have it.

She and Charlie put their arms around each other on the couch. Then she puts one of her feet on top of his feet. I try not to stare. Sam's able to act like it's normal that Lucy's here. Normal that Charlie has a girlfriend.

ON FRIDAY MORNING NETTIE has asked to see Kit and me without Sam. She places the clipboard in her lap again when we get there. It takes Kit some time to maneuver the crutches and sit down on the couch next to me. I take in the smell of him— the earthiness and something almost lemon. Nettie asks us if Sam seems calmer now.

I say, "Less stormy, maybe, I think."

"He's going to figure all this out," she says. "But the first thing we want is for him to not smoke pot at school."

"That would be a good start." Kit laughs and puts his hand on my knee and I leave it there.

"The pot is part of the guilt," she says. "It's not the real problem." She pulls her feet up under her in the chair. "Your accident set off something in him, Kit. And maybe in you too?"

"I'm sure not here to talk about myself." He smiles.

She acts like she hasn't heard him. "Does either of you have anything in your own lives to compare it to?"

Kit says, "Compare what to?"

"Sam's pain. His trauma."

"I think that word's extreme."

Nettie says, "Then let's not use it, but I think you know what's going on here, Kit. We're talking about guilt and grief and how we carry them forward."

He looks up at the ceiling. "I don't really know what you're talking about. I don't know about carrying things forward. I'm one of those survivors you hear about. People like me don't go over the past. I mean I think Sam gets sad and he's partying more now, but that's normal. Sam will be just fine."

Nettie doesn't say anything for a moment. Then she says, "We're only here today to try to help Sam."

Kit says, "So what are you really asking me?"

Nettie smiles and looks right at him. "Maybe to try and see your son differently. One of the greatest casualties in trauma is the loss of vulnerability. I don't want Sam to keep wanting to numb himself. I want him to dare to be vulnerable. I want to hear how you and Jill process pain and trauma. Oops. There's that word again. And you don't have to talk, Kit, if this is too uncomfortable. I'm not here to make you tell me your secrets. That's not my job. That's not why I became a therapist."

"Jesus." He shakes his head and smiles.

I can tell it's still his instinct to go it alone. It's always been his instinct. But he looks at me and I take his hand.

"Okay. My mother died when I was ten. I was with her when she had a stroke in our kitchen. Is that what you want?"

She doesn't act like she heard any of his aggression.

I squeeze his hand.

"I don't know what could be more extreme," Nettie says and some of her hair slips from her braid. She moves it out of her eyes. "Than watching someone you love die."

She lets that sit. Then she says, "Or almost dying yourself on a boat."

Kit rubs the side of his face, but I don't think he's aware he's doing it. "I don't know why you think this is related to Sam. I just don't follow you."

"And you think about your mother how often now?" Nettie chews on the end of her pen.

"All the time, really." He laughs. "You've got me there." Then he rolls his eyes like Sam does when he's cornered.

All the time? He thinks about his mother all the time?

"She's on the boat with me. It's hard not to think about her out there. I get this feeling that she's coming back." He smiles.

Nettie smiles back at him. "Sam can't stop thinking about Liam. You take your mother on your boat. I bet Jill didn't know that."

I say, "I hate that I didn't know."

"And what about Jill?" Nettie says. "Why haven't you told her?"

He laughs. "Well, I mean it's crazy. Talking to my dead mother on my boat."

"Ah," Nettie says. "So it stays safe if you don't talk about it? What's the feeling you get now?"

"The feeling?"

"What does it feel like when you think about that day your mother died?"

He exhales slowly and makes a whistling sound. "Cold. Alone. I couldn't save her. Then she left."

Nettie nods. "She left you. I see. And do you ever have that feeling now?"

"Ha." He smiles and puts his head back and closes his eyes. "What is this? This is like some cross-examination." He turns and stares at me like maybe I planned this. But I just shake my head at him.

Nettie repeats the question and smiles, like she has all the time in the world. "I'm just curious, Kit. For no real reason, but do you ever have that feeling of being alone now?"

"Well, all the time in the hospital," he says. "All the freaking time."

"You were alone there?"

"After Jill left. She had to come back to be with the boys. I understood it, but—"

"You needed her to stay so you wouldn't feel alone?"

He's quiet again. Then he says, "I get it now. I get what you're trying to do here."

"I have no ulterior motive, Kit. None. I just want you to talk about what it felt like in the hospital after Jill was gone."

I'm holding my breath. I hold it. Then I let it out as quietly as I can. Then I take another breath and hold it again.

"Did you ask Jill to stay?"

He's quiet for a second. Then he rubs his eyes with his hand. "I didn't think I needed to."

It looks like some kind of punishment now, what I did to him. There's the unexpectedness of it, and there's my guilt, which I give in to. When I breathe normally the tears come, and they're a relief after holding my breath.

WE'RE BOTH QUIET ON the ride home. I drive slowly, without the radio, and when we get to the house, I sit in the car with him and close my eyes and wait for what happens next. Maybe he knows.

He stares at the A-frame. Stares and stares at it.

Then he says, "Do you know how much I hate living here?"

"Hate what?"

"Hate this house."

What is he saying?

"I've always hated it. For as long as I remember."

"I thought you wanted to live here."

He laughs. "I'd do anything to get out of here."

I'm so surprised that I start laughing. "God, I'm sorry. I didn't mean to laugh."

"I know it's crazy."

"Then why do we come here?"

"Because I'm messed in the head? Because I thought I could handle it? I don't know. Because we need a place to stay? There's so much guilt in this house. I couldn't save her. God, I tried. I couldn't."

"You were ten, Kit."

Lara has a bumper sticker on her car that says CHANGE OR DIE. It reminds her to always be open.

"I'm so sorry you feel this way about the house. Thank you for telling me. Thank you. I'm really glad you told me." Then I lean over and take his hand.

Marriage is long, and you have to will yourself to choose it. Change or die.

"Told you what? That I can't get over my mother's death?"

"I just wish you'd told me sooner. I've been right here."

"I don't want to live here anymore. That's the first thing I want to change." He looks at me. "There's more."

"I'm sure there is."

"I wasn't myself up there. Things got away from me, Jilly." His skin is ruddier now, and he looks much healthier.

"Can we not do this now?" We just got back from Nettie's. My head's spinning.

"But I've been waiting to say it. You've got to give this to me. She didn't know me. I propped myself up a little with it. Marsh didn't understand my problems. She was a friend. That's all. It's not an excuse."

"Could we never say her name again? Never?" I look away at the house.

"I'm here now. You know I am, Jilly. It was only ever you. Only you."

Then he reaches around my shoulder and pulls me closer to him.

He says, "Nettie can really mess with your head."

His eyes are glistening, and the blue in them shines because of the sunlight off the windshield.

I lean back in my seat and close my eyes and keep holding on to his hand.

JIMMY FINDS ME IN the kitchen a few hours later and says the blizzard he's been tracking on the Weather Channel is going to hit by eight tonight. He's bought most of the D batteries at Candy's and puts them on the table in a big Ziploc bag. Then he gets out the four flashlights from the cupboard above the fridge. He wants me to replace all the batteries in the flashlights while he watches.

"Right now?" I'm almost done making the beef stew with red wine Kit loves. "What about Kit? He's better at flashlights than me."

Kit's in the living room trying to fix the storm window next to the couch.

Jimmy says the power will be out by midnight, and he's going to watch me put all these new batteries in right now. "Do it while you can. Don't wait. That's the only way we'll know if they work."

I unscrew the first flashlight and take out the dead batteries. Then I say, "Thank you for worrying about us." I mean it.

He stands by the stove, hands in pockets, and acts like he hasn't heard me. He keeps his eyes on the flashlight.

I put the first batteries in.

"No, not like that. The other ends need to touch." He takes the flashlight and reverses the batteries and screws the end on, then hands me the next one.

"Now you try. How's your movie, by the way? You got an ending yet?"

I smile. None of my films really have endings even though they do have to end.

"I'm waiting to see what happens."

"I don't believe in happy endings anyway," he says.

I stare at him. "Jimmy. Me either. I really want you in the film. Will you think about it?"

He hands me another flashlight and shakes his head. "You never give up, do you?"

Kit comes into the hallway on the crutches and says the window won't budge. He's wearing an old green crewneck sweater of Sam's. It makes him look like the boy at the lodge that first summer.

He tells Jimmy that Shorty wants to sell his own boat and go in on Kit's trawler with him and focus on flounder and haddock, because those stocks have rebounded and between the two men they have some quota.

Jimmy says that might make sense. "Just take care of your boat, son. Your boat has to bring you home safely at the end of the day."

He walks toward the stairs. "Which window is it? Come show me. I'll take a crack at it."

I go upstairs and find an old crocheted dress in the closet in Kit's room that my mother made me when I was sixteen and put it on over my jeans. It's not my style anymore, but I have an urge to be someone else today.

CHARLIE COMES HOME AT six and sees me in the dress and says he's not sure.

"Not sure about what?" I finish slicing the tomatoes and put them on top of the salad and hand him the bowl.

"The whole dress-over-pants thing."

"Not sure in general, or on me?"

"Both," he says. "I'm sorry to report."

Kit comes in and says he likes the dress.

We look at each other and there's that recognition. Oh. There you are. I've been waiting for you.

Jimmy waves at us and shakes his head and leaves.

Sam comes up from Shorty's pier and stays quiet on the subject of my dress over my pants.

I'm watching him but trying just to let him be in his Clash T-shirt with the flag of hair.

The boys and I bring the bowls of stew into the living room, and Kit edges way back on the bed until he's leaning against the wall, then he takes his bowl from Sam and starts eating.

Charlie tells us that he's made his decision on robots.

"I didn't know we were waiting on one." Kit laughs.

"We don't need them," Charlie says. "I don't need them. Do you, Dad? Life is already good without robots. But they will happen. Robots are already happening. Just wait until they figure out time travel."

"Who is they?" I ask him.

"The robots," Charlie says.

"The robots are going to figure out time travel?" I say.

"Charlie, you're losing it." Sam smiles, but it's not a mean smile.

"They'll do it, and it will be terrible," Charlie says. "Imagine having to experience being an infant again and everything you felt? No. I want to die before I have to do that." He drains all the water in his glass. "We have to figure out what to do when the sun explodes. Because it's happening. It's really happening. I hope I'm not reincarnated to a life on Mars. Because that's going to be very complicated. Very hard."

"Wow," Kit says. "It does sound hard."

Charlie points at Sam. "What's that?"

"What's what?"

"That dirt above your lip?"

"Shut up, Charlie," Sam says.

"Oh my God. It's a mustache," Charlie says.

"No, really, Charlie, stop," Sam says.

"Sam, take it off. Please take it off." Charlie's laughing now.

Sam says nothing, but he's still smiling at us.

"No, seriously, take it off right now," Charlie says.

"I support you." Kit smiles at Sam. "I support you in your attempt to grow a mustache."

SAM GOES UP TO the bathroom after dinner and doesn't come out for almost an hour.

Charlie bangs on the door and says he's wetting his pants.

But Sam won't open the door. "There is a toilet downstairs, Charlie."

When he finally comes out, he doesn't have a starter mustache anymore. But he's laughing.

"God." He flings himself down next to Charlie on the couch. "That looked awful. Why didn't any of you tell me how bad?"

They are my people. All three of them.

I could stand in this hallway and stare at them for hours and not grow tired of it.

*ACKNOWLEDGMENTS*

First I want to thank my mother, Thorne Conley, for all her kindnesses and generosity and for showing me how to live in the Maine woods without shutting the rest of the world out.

This book was written thanks to many other people too: My father, Mike Conley, who showed me the meaning of family and of appreciating the simpler life down a long dirt road. My brother and sister, John Conley and Erin Conley, without whom I would be no one.

Dearest first readers, Caitlin Gutheil, Anja Hanson, Lily King, Maryanne O'Hara.

Dearest editor and friend, Carole Baron. You've taught me so much about writing and living with purpose, and big-heartedness, and delight for the world. It could fill another book.

The incomparable team at Knopf: Rob Shapiro, you're a dream to work with, thank you for getting this book from the start. Bette Alexander, who carried the book so valiantly through the pandemic. Lydia Buechler and Maria Massey, who were so extraordinary and generous in this upside-down time. So too, Emily Reardon and Julianne Clancy, to whom I'm indebted. Also Nick Latimer for everything he does so very superbly, all over again. Kelly Blair, for the extraordinary jacket design, and Maria Carella for the truly special interior design.

My deeply wise and compassionate agent, Stephanie Cabot, who read an early draft three years ago and never stopped cheering for it.

Thanks also to the many people who know more about commercial fishing in Maine than I do, and who over the years have shared their knowledge so generously: the late and terribly missed Danny Kaler, David Norton, Ben Martens of the Maine Coast Fisherman's Association, Merritt Carey, and the other Maine fishermen who kindly spent time with me.

My friends and colleagues at the Stonecoast Writing Program who kindly listened to me read works-in-progress from the book over the years and rooted for it.

And finally: Tony and Thorne and Aidan. It's for you three. Always.

## A Note About the Author

Susan Conley grew up in Maine. She is the author of four previous books, including *Elsey Come Home*. Her writing has appeared in *The New York Times Magazine, The Paris Review,* the *Virginia Quarterly Review, The New York Times,* the *Harvard Review,* the *New England Review,* and *Ploughshares.* She has received multiple fellowships from the MacDowell Colony as well fellowships from the Bread Loaf Writers' Conference, the Maine Arts Commission, and the Massachusetts Art Commission. She has won the Maine Literary Award and the Maine Award for Publishing Excellence. She is a founder of the Telling Room, a youth creative writing center in Portland, Maine, where she lives and teaches on the faculty of the Stonecoast Writers Program.

## A Note on the Type

This book was set in Granjon, a type named in compliment to Robert Granjon, a type cutter and printer active in Antwerp, Lyons, Rome, and Paris from 1523 to 1590. Granjon, the boldest and most original designer of his time, was one of the first to practice the trade of typefounder apart from that of printer.

Linotype Granjon was designed by George W. Jones, who based his drawings on a face used by Claude Garamond (ca. 1480–1561) in his beautiful French books. Granjon more closely resembles Garamond's own type than do any of the various modern faces that bear his name.

Typeset by Scribe, Philadelphia, Pennsylvania
Printed and bound by Berryville Graphics, Berryville,
     Virginia
Designed by Maria Carella